RESISTANCE

**In a Nazi-occupied Ireland,
where would you stand?**

Brian Gallagher

THE O'BRIEN PRESS
DUBLIN

First published 2019 by The O'Brien Press Ltd,
12 Terenure Road East, Rathgar, Dublin 6, D06 HD27, Ireland.
Tel: +353 1 4923333; Fax: +353 1 4922777
E-mail: books@obrien.ie
Website: www.obrien.ie
The O'Brien Press is a member of Publishing Ireland.

ISBN: 978-1-78849-080-1

7 6 5 4 3 2 1
22 21 20 19

Printed and bound by CPI Group (UK) Ltd, Croydon, CR0 4YY.
The paper in this book is produced using pulp from managed forests.

Published in:

DUBLIN
UNESCO
City of Literature

DEDICATION

To Miriam – thanks for being the greatest supporter that any writer could ever hope to have.

ACKNOWLEDGEMENTS

My thanks to Michael O'Brien for supporting the idea of a novel dealing with Operation Green, the plan for a Nazi invasion of Ireland, to my editor, Helen Carr, for her excellent editing and advice, to publicists Ruth Heneghan and Ruth Ennis for all their efforts on my behalf, to Emma Byrne for her superb work on cover design, and to the everyone at O'Brien Press, with whom it's a pleasure to work.

My thanks also go to Hugh McCusker for his expert proof-reading, to Claire and Domhnall Fahey for assiatance with German translation, and to Oisin O'Donovan-Kelly, a young reader who shared with me his views of an early draft of the story.

My sincere thanks go to Fingal Arts Office for their bursary support.

And finally, my deepest thanks are for the constant encouragement of my family, Miriam, Orla and Mark, and Peter and Shelby.

PROLOGUE

MONDAY, 3 FEBRUARY 1941

SACRED HEART CONVENT,
CORK CITY

achel felt a sense of dread as she looked down the avenue. The sky was blue, and the air mild, on this the first day of spring. Rachel, though, couldn't suppress a shiver as she watched the sleek, black car that was coming up the tree-lined avenue from the main road. It was flying a swastika, the Nazi flag that flew on public buildings all over Ireland since the invasion the previous autumn, when the Germans had bloodily overwhelmed the Irish army and occupied the country within a week.

Rachel watched the car intently, hoping that it would turn right at the fork in the avenue. Left would bring the vehicle towards the primary school where she was a pupil, whereas right would mean its destination was the secondary school. On reaching the fork, the car turned left and Rachel felt her stomach tightening. *Don't panic*, she told herself. *It may be nothing to do with you*. But she was the only girl in the school from a Jewish background, and the Germans had been rounding up Irish Jews and putting them into concentration camps. The Nazis often worked in tandem with the local *Gardaí*, but the Irish police were very much the junior partner, and all the power lay with the German Secret Police, the much-feared *Gestapo*.

Rachel turned away and walked quickly across the noisy schoolyard. It was breaktime, and the yard was full of uniformed girls, the younger ones excitedly playing chasing. From the corner of her eye Rachel saw the car pulling to a halt. She glanced backwards and saw two men getting out of the vehicle. One was in a *Garda* uniform, but the other man was in civilian clothes and wore a long black coat, despite the mild weather. Definitely *Gestapo*, thought Rachel, quickening her pace. She was tempted to run back to her classroom, grab her belongings and make for the rear exit of the grounds. Instead she forced herself not to draw attention and walked at a brisk pace towards the school's reception area. She entered the main hall, the smell of beeswax polish hanging in the air.

There were other pupils about, and Rachel made sure not to catch the eye of Mrs Rafferty, the middle-aged woman who ran the school office. If the policemen *were* looking for her, the last thing she wanted was Mrs Rafferty to identify her. Rachel stopped and tried to think clearly. Was she getting herself into a state over nothing? Perhaps she should loiter in the hall, writing in a copybook while eavesdropping to hear the policemen's business at the reception desk. Rachel hesitated, then her instincts kicked in and she decided to put as much distance as possible between herself and the police. If she took her belongings from the classroom and left the school, and it was all a false alarm, so what? Better to get in trouble with Sister Carmel than to end up in the clutches of the *Gestapo*.

Without further delay she turned into the corridor and made for her classroom. On reaching the door to the room, she swung it open and stepped inside. She collected her coat from the rack and was halfway to her desk when she found that she wasn't alone.

'What are you doing?' said a voice.

Rachel turned around, startled. 'Sister Carmel,' she said, realis-

10

ing that her teacher had been at the back of the classroom

'Why are you here during breaktime?' asked the nun.

'I…I came for my bag and coat.'

'Why?'

Rachel looked at the nun, unsure what to tell her. Sister Carmel taught maths and religion and was regarded by the girls as strict, but fair. But her manner wasn't sympathetic, and Rachel had never warmed to her.

'You're trying my patience, Rachel,' said the nun.

'Sorry, sister, I…'

'What?'

'I'm frightened.'

'Frightened of what?'

'That…that the Nazis are coming for me. They've arrested all the Jews they could find in Cork.'

'But your mother wasn't detected. So the chances of them coming for you—'

'They're here! Two policemen are in reception!' said Rachel, for once daring to interrupt her teacher mid-sentence.

Part of her hoped that Sister Carmel would reprimand her for interrupting, and would tell her that the visit had nothing to do with her. Instead the nun looked concerned.

'Did you hear what they said to Mrs Rafferty?' she asked.

'No, I was afraid to hang about in case I'd be spotted.'

'Right.'

'Can I leave, Sister? Please. I'll come back tomorrow if it's all a big mistake.'

Sister Carmel looked uncertain, then she nodded. 'All right.'

Just then they heard the sound of footsteps approaching along the corridor.

Rachel looked at Sister Carmel aware that the heavy tread wasn't being made by schoolgirls. 'This could be them!' she said.

Sister Carmel looked frightened, then seemed to make a snap decision. 'Quickly, Rachel,' she whispered, 'into the broom cupboard!'

Rachel grabbed her schoolbag and ran across the room. She entered the tall storage cupboard and closed the door after her. She lowered her schoolbag and coat to the ground then stood still, her heart pounding. No sooner had she settled herself than she heard a loud knock on the classroom door, followed by the sound of the door being opened.

'May I help you?' she heard Sister Carmel ask in a strong, confident voice.

Rachel had seen the fear in the nun's eyes, however, and she wondered if her teacher could keep her nerve long enough to outwit the police. The *Gestapo* had a reputation for brutality, and being a nun wouldn't save her if they took her in for interrogation.

Rachel heard footsteps as the two men approached, and she peeped through a crack in the side of the door.

'I'm sorry to disturb you, Sister. I'm Sergeant Moran, and this is *Kriminalkommissar* Vogts.'

Rachel saw that Sergeant Moran had wavy, ginger hair and an

open, almost friendly expression. *Kriminalkommissar* Vogts was ath-letically built, with tightly cropped brown hair, and his demeanour seemed more threatening.

'We want one of your pupils,' said the German in accented but fluent English.

The man's tone was less courteous than the Irish policeman's, and Rachel felt her knees beginning to tremble. Could there be some reason why they might want to talk to another pupil? But even as she clung to the slim hope, her worst fears were founded by Vogts.

'We wish to see Rachel Clarke,' he said.

'May I ask why?'

'No, you may not,' said Vogts sharply. 'Where is she?'

Rachel's heart was pounding madly, and she found herself hold-ing her breath. Sister Carmel was strict when it came to religious instruction, and she had taught the girls that a lie is always sinful. Would she lie now to save a pupil? And even if she *was* prepared to commit a sin, would she risk bringing the wrath of the *Gestapo* down on the school for the sake of one girl?

'I couldn't say where exactly she is,' said Sister Carmel.

Despite her own terror, Rachel felt a surge of admiration for her teacher.

'You couldn't say, or you won't say?' said Vogts.

'I couldn't say. She didn't come in today.'

'Really?'

'Yes.'

'Why not?'

'I don't know.'

'Is she usually a good attender?'

'Yes.'

'Yet the one day we want to see her, she's not here?'

'Perhaps she knew you were coming.'

'How would she know that?' queried Sergeant Moran.

'I've no way of telling, seeing as I don't know why you want her,' retorted Sister Carmel.

'We want her because she's Jewish,' said Vogts bluntly.

Despite Rachel knowing this had to be the reason for their visit, hearing it said aloud was chilling. Terrible stories had reached Ireland of what the Nazis were doing to Jews in Europe, and she felt herself trembling with fear.

'There must be some mistake,' said Sister Carmel. 'Rachel Clarke is a practising Catholic. She'll be making her Confirmation next month.'

'All that proves is how devious these Jews are,' answered Vogts. 'Her mother was Judith Goldberg before she married Edward Clarke and took his name.'

'Be that as it may, Rachel Clarke is a practising Catholic.'

'To mislead people. But when it comes to race, the child of a Jewish mother is Jewish. That's the law.'

'That hasn't been the way in Ireland. Has it, sergeant?'

'I'm…I'm sorry, Sister. Things have changed.'

'It's the law of the *Reich*,' said Vogts. 'Anyone guilty of obstructing it faces severe punishment. So I ask you again. And think carefully before you answer. Where is Rachel Clarke?'

Rachel swallowed hard, pressing her knees together to try to stop the trembling.

'I don't know Rachel's precise location,' said Sister Carmel.

'But you have an idea where she might be. Better if you co-operate,' said Vogts threateningly. 'For you, the school, the Sacred Heart order.'

Rachel bit her lip. The school and the order were the core of Sister Carmel's being. Even if she was willing to risk her own life, would she put the school and the order at risk for one pupil?

'All right then,' the nun answered.

'Where is she?'

Sister Carmel paused, then spoke reluctantly. 'I imagine she's in England.'

'England?'

'She has family there. Probably the Clarkes saw this coming and she fled. There are ferries every day. She could have left from Cork, or Rosslare, or even Dublin. Have you taken her parents into custody, Sergeant?'

Before the Irish policeman could respond, Vogts cut in, 'We don't discuss police matters with civilians.'

'As you wish. Well…if there isn't anything else, Gentlemen, I have classes to prepare for.'

There was a pause, and Rachel prayed that the policemen would leave. To Rachel's ears Sister Carmel had sounded convincing, but there was no telling how the *Gestapo* officer would respond.

'Right, so. Thank you for your time, Sister,' said Sergeant Moran.

'Very well,' said Vogts. 'That is all – for now.'

Rachel silently breathed out, hugely relieved that they were leaving. But she still had to get out of the school, and there was the terrifying thought that her parents might already be arrested. Right now, though, she had to put that from her mind, and concentrate on safely exiting the convent grounds.

'I'll see you to reception,' said Sister Carmel, and Rachel realised that the nun was giving her a chance to emerge from the broom cupboard as she escorted the policemen back to the entrance hall.

Rachel stood unmoving, even after she heard the classroom door closing and the sound of the policemen's footsteps fading away. In the space of a few minutes her world had been turned upside down, and the fear that gripped her was paralysing. But she couldn't stay here. She needed to move, and quickly. Steeling herself, she stepped out of the broom cupboard and crossed to the classroom door.

Rachel peered out carefully, relieved to see that there was no sign of Sergeant Moran or *Kriminalkommissar* Vogts in the corridor. She slung her schoolbag onto her back, draped her coat over her arm, and then walked swiftly down the corridor in the opposite direction to reception. Being breaktime, she didn't encounter any other students, and she quickly turned out of the corridor and out the rear door of the building to the entrance to the bicycle shed. She moved to her bike and unlocked it, then donned her coat. Her heart was still pounding and she dreaded to think what might have happened to her parents. *Well, the sooner she got out of the school, the sooner she'd know.* Mounting the bicycle, she headed for the lane that acted as a back entrance to the convent grounds. She rounded the corner of the bicycle shed, rose out of the saddle, then cycled away at speed.

PART ONE

MAY 1943

OCCUPATION

CHAPTER ONE

RAINBOW RESTAURANT, O'CONNELL STREET, DUBLIN.

Kevin Burke felt angry. He knew it was pointless, but he couldn't help himself. Every time he travelled down O'Connell Street, it struck him anew. Although there was little that a twelve-year-old boy could do to change things, he still felt sickened when he saw the Nazi swastika flying over the General

Post Office, where the Irish tricolour used to fly.

It was over two years since Ireland and Britain had fallen to the Nazis, but it still grated with Kevin to see German soldiers occupying his country. The war that Adolf Hitler had started in 1939 by invading Poland was still going on, with fierce battles taking place between the Russians and the Germans on the Eastern Front. In Western Europe, however, France, Belgium and Holland had fallen quickly to the Nazis, followed by a bloody, but successful, invasion of Britain and Ireland in the autumn of 1940. Despite Ireland being a neutral country, and the Irish army putting up a brave fight, the Nazis had ruthlessly overwhelmed all resistance, and within a week of the fall of Britain, Ireland too was under Nazi rule.

The Irish leader, Éamon de Valera, led a government-in-exile in Washington, while Britain's Prime Minister, Winston Churchill, had escaped to Canada, from where he too was opposing the Nazis. Meanwhile, people in Ireland survived as best they could, with German law enforced by the *Gestapo*, any form of resistance brutally suppressed, and food strictly rationed. Bread, meat, fish, butter, sugar and tea were all in short supply to the general population, and required ration coupons for their purchase.

Kevin looked across the Rainbow Restaurant now, as smartly dressed waiters served the guests. His anger was giving way to guilt. The air carried the delicious smell of roasted meat, and a pianist was softly playing in the background. But why should he and his parents eat fine food in fancy surroundings when so many people in Ireland were going without? The discomforting answer was that as well as being a successful auctioneer, his father was also a member of Dublin Corporation. The Nazis had total control of Irish life, with an all-powerful *Reich-Protector* dictating German policy. But it suited the Nazis to have local politicians handling the day-to-day running of the city, and with that came certain privileges.

With Ireland being an agricultural country, much of its output was now exported to feed the German army. Generous allowance was made, however, for selected Irish restaurants where German officers dined, and access to these venues was one of the most valued benefits offered to local politicians.

'Cheer up, Kevin, it might never happen!' said his father playfully, breaking Kevin's reverie.

'Sorry, I…I was miles away,' Kevin answered, trying for a grin.

It was his mother's birthday today, and the three of them had come into town to celebrate. His father wore a well-tailored three-piece suit, and his mother wore a blue satin dress. For her sake, Kevin had kept his misgivings to himself, and now he turned to her. 'How is your fish, Mam?'

'Lovely, thanks.'

'Fresh from the trawlers in Howth,' said Dad. 'And the chef here is excellent. That's a winning combo.'

Kevin nodded agreeably. He wanted his mother to have a nice birthday – he'd given her a home-made birthday card and a charcoal drawing he had done of the Royal Canal – and he resolved to make more of an effort to hide his feelings.

They finished their main courses, then Kevin looked up with curiosity as a German officer approached their table. He was a middle-aged man in a smartly-cut uniform. By now, Kevin could tell the difference between *SS* officers with their black uniforms and swastika armbands, *Luftwaffe* pilots in their light blue uniforms, and regular army men in their uniforms of grey, which this man wore.

'Major Weber,' said Kevin's father, rising to his feet and offering his hand.

'Councillor Burke. Good to see you,' said the German in clipped English.

'This is my wife, Una,' said Dad.

'A pleasure to meet you *Frau* Burke,' said Weber, bowing slightly before shaking hands.

'And this is my son, Kevin.'

Kevin rose. He hated being polite to those who were occupying Ireland – and ruthlessly executing anyone who opposed them – but good manners dictated that he be courteous. He reached out to shake the German's hand. As an only child he was used to meeting adults, and normally he would have engaged in conversation. But although he had to shake hands, he was determined not to make small talk with a Nazi.

'A fine boy,' said Weber, shaking hands and patting Kevin on the shoulder.

Keep your hands to yourself! Kevin felt like shouting, but he contented himself with giving no reaction whatsoever.

If Weber had picked up on Kevin's lack of a response he didn't show it. 'I don't wish to intrude,' he said, his English fluent despite the clipped delivery.

'Not at all,' said Dad.

'No, indeed,' added Mam, with a polite smile.

Kevin knew his father generally altered his demeanour to fit the company in which he found himself. But while Dad had no choice but to deal with these people, Kevin still wished his parents would be a bit more reserved with Weber.

'No, it's a family occasion,' said the German. 'I just wanted to say good evening. And also to say that I look forward to your cooperation, Councillor, regarding the shipment to Hamburg next week.'

'Which you'll certainly have, Major.'

'Excellent. Well, *Frau* Burke, Kevin,' said the officer, nodding in farewell.

Kevin hated being called by his first name, as though Weber was a family friend, but he joined his mother in saying goodbye. Then the German returned to a table of officers at the far side of the busy room.

'Who is he, Tom?' asked his mother.

'Major Conrad Weber. Quite an important person.'

'Nice of him to come over.'

'He's one of the more civilised ones. Though he was also putting on a little pressure.'

'Oh? How's that?

'There's a big consignment of beef to go to Hamburg next week. We have to handle the paperwork. He was marking my cards that he wants no snags at our end.'

'Ah.'

'But I've always kept on the right side of him, so we get on. Talking of which…' Kevin's father turned and looked at him questioningly.

'What?' said Kevin.

'You could have been a bit friendlier.'

'Friendlier?'

'Yes. You were borderline rude, Kevin. He probably thinks you were just shy, but you could have made an effort.'

Kevin felt his hackles rise but he made sure to lower his voice. 'You want me to be friends with people who are murderers?'

'Kevin!' said his mother.

'Major Weber isn't a murderer,' said his father in a low voice.

'They kill hostages, Dad, they kill Resistance fighters, they kill Jews.'

'Major Weber is a quartermaster. He organises food supplies.'

'So he feeds the ones who do the killing.'

His father hesitated, then spoke again, his voice still low. 'Perhaps he does. But I can't change that. So what would you have me do, Kevin? Condemn the Nazis? And end up before a firing squad? Or in a concentration camp – and maybe you and Mam along with me?'

Kevin didn't have an answer, but his father held his gaze.

'What would you have me do, son?' he said gently.

'I…I don't know, Dad.'

To Kevin's surprise, his father reached out and squeezed his hand. 'These are desperate times, Kevin. We do what we have to do, and try to muddle through. All right?'

'All right, Dad.'

But if you muddled through alongside people who committed murder, at what stage did you become part of the process?

'Anyway, that's enough of the gloom,' said Mam, with forced cheerfulness. 'Apple crumble for desert, Kevin?'

'Yes,' he answered, trying to sound upbeat for his mother's sake. 'Apple crumble for desert.'

Mary Flanagan kept her head down and strode past Tierneys' house, hoping not to be seen. Normally she enjoyed being with Roisin Tierney, who had become her neighbour and friend on moving to Dublin two years ago. Now, though, Mary needed to be alone, and she kept up her brisk pace as she turned out of Shandon Park and made for Phibsboro Road.

Mary carried a small basket of flowers for her father's grave and she turned left on reaching the main road. It was a short walk from here to Glasnevin Cemetery, and the late afternoon sunshine bathed the city in warm, golden light. The pocket gardens of the houses along her route were ablaze with colour, with flowers, shrubs, and potted plants thriving in the early summer heat. Mary thought that May was the best month of the year, and she loved the bright green of the leaves when they unfolded after their long, winter hibernation.

Mary savoured the scented air, then her sense of wellbeing was shattered by a volley of shots. She jumped slightly, taken by surprise even though she knew what the firing meant. *More executions in the prison yard of Mountjoy Jail.*

The Germans routinely executed captured Resistance fighters, which was brutal but unsurprising. What had cowed people far more, however, was the willingness of the Nazis to execute black marketeers, trade union officials, rebel priests – in fact anyone who dared to resist Hitler's occupation of the country.

Mary's family had first-hand experience of the ruthlessness of the occupiers. Her mother's Widow's Pension had been stopped by the authorities because Commandant Flanagan was among those officers who had continued irregular warfare after the Irish army had been forced to surrender to the invading Germans.

Luckily her parents owned the house in Shandon Park, so Mary and her siblings had a roof over their heads. Mam had been forced to go back to her original career of dressmaking, however, and even now, two years later, money was scarce.

Still, there were millions of people all over Europe in far worse situations, Mary reminded herself, as she stepped through the main gates of the cemetery. She passed the tall round tower that was both a tomb and a monument to the great Daniel O'Connell, after whom the main street of Dublin was named. O'Connell had been a political leader who believed in bringing about change by non-violent means, which Mary had always admired. *But how would someone like O'Connell cope when faced with a violent tyrant such as Adolf Hitler?*

There was no easy answer, and Mary put the question from her mind for now as she made her way deeper into the cemetery. The overhanging trees created a cool and shady atmosphere, and Mary met few other mourners as she approached the distant corner of the cemetery where the Flanagan family plot was.

Looking around, she saw nobody in sight, and she stepped forward and placed her flowers on the grave. She gazed once more at the headstone, even though she knew its message almost off by heart:

Pray for the soul of Commandant Patrick (Paddy) Flanagan, born 1899, died 1941. A proud Irishman and a loving husband and father. RIP.

'Are you not going to say a prayer for the deceased?'

Mary spun around. The man who had silently slipped out from behind the nearby trees had a wry smile.

'You put the heart crossways in me!' said Mary.

'Sorry, love. Have you got a hug for your aul' dad?'

Mary grinned and quickly moved forward, dropping her basket and wrapping her arms around her father. He held her close for a moment, and she realised that although he was still a big, powerful man – his father and grandfather had been blacksmiths – he was thinner than he used to be, and she hoped he was getting enough to eat. She realised too – as she always did on their meetings – how much she missed him. But not having him at home was the price she paid for having a father who was a senior figure in the Resistance. And even though she sometimes missed him really badly, Mary had to admit that it was a brilliant piece of deception to have staged a fake funeral.

It had taken place after a bloody clash in the early days of the occupation between the Germans and remnants of the Irish Army that had continued to fight, and it meant that although the *Gestapo* were constantly hunting for Resistance leaders, the name of Paddy Flanagan was never on their list. It was a big sacrifice for the family not to have their father at home, but his apparent death kept them free from official notice, while he lived in the shadows, frequently moving from safe house to safe house.

'How's Mam?' he asked now as he released Mary.

'She's grand. Always keeps the best side out.'

'And the girls?'

'Fine. Gretta lost her front baby teeth, and she threw a glass of water over Deirdre for calling her Gummy Gretta!'

Da smiled, but Mary thought she saw a sadness in his eyes, and she guessed that it must pain him to miss seeing his children growing up.

'So,' said her father, 'got anything for me?'

'Yes,' answered Mary, reaching for her basket. 'A few rock buns. Mam got her hands on some flour.'

'Lovely.'

'And this,' said Mary, handing over a large manila envelope.

'Good girl,' said her father, taking the envelope and placing it in his jacket pocket.

'Any messages you need me to pass on?' she asked.

'No, love, not this time. Just…'

'*Be careful in the extreme* – I know, Dad,' said Mary with a smile.

'Sorry, I know I repeat myself. I hate…I hate involving you at all, Mary.'

'Please, Dad. We've gone over this. *You* need someone you can trust. *I* want to help.'

'All right,' said her father, raising his hand in surrender, 'all right.'

'So, any outside news?' asked Mary, knowing her father often knew about developments before they became common knowledge.

'Yes, actually. Winston Churchill is addressing the US Congress today.'

Mary was unsure how a speech from the British Prime Minister-in-exile might matter, and she looked at her father enquiringly. 'Is that good for us?'

'It is. Churchill has never been a friend to Ireland, but there's a saying in war. "Your enemy's enemy is your friend." And Winston Churchill is Adolf Hitler's enemy.'

'So now he's our friend?'

'Not exactly. But it's good if he persuades the Americans to commit more to fighting the Nazis.'

'To help free Ireland?'

'Yes. The Americans are mostly fighting Japan. If it wasn't for the Russians, the Nazis would have a free hand in Europe. But if the British and the Americans launch an invasion in the West, while Hitler is bogged down fighting the Russians in the East, then there's a chance for all of us.'

'Right,' said Mary thoughtfully. 'Then let's pray that Mr Churchill succeeds,'

'Amen to that, Mary,' said her father gravely. 'Amen to that.'

CHAPTER TWO

oisin Tierney sat on a hard, wooden chair in Phibsboro Youth Club, quietly fuming. She hated how the Nazis influenced every aspect of Irish life with schools, hospitals, sports organisations and even her local youth club answerable to the occupying power. She particularly loathed the Hitler Youth movement, whose Irish teenage members strutted the streets of Dublin in their Nazi uniforms.

Tonight one of them was giving a talk to the assembled members of the club, and the sunny evening was making the room stuffy and uncomfortably warm. Roisin looked across at her friends, Kevin and Mary. Mary's face gave nothing away, but Kevin was making little effort to hide his boredom as the Hitler Youth speaker droned on about German values.

Sitting behind her friends was Dennis O'Sullivan, a boy Roisin had never liked, and it seemed to Roisin that he was actually interested in what was being said. *How could anyone swallow German propaganda,* she thought, *when the Nazis inflicted misery on millions of people?* And yet in every occupied country in Europe there had been those who collaborated with the enemy. Ireland was no exception, and Roisin knew that a minority of Irish people were willing collaborators, another minority were active in the Resistance, while most people kept their heads down and tried to survive.

Finally the talk came to an end, and Mr Cox, an easy-going local shop-keeper who ran the youth club, lead the applause. Roisin didn't hold this against Mr Cox – if he offended the Nazis they would probably shut down his shop – and she applauded herself, without enthusiasm, yet not so grudgingly as to draw attention.

The story of my life, she thought, *do nothing to draw attention.* It had been drummed into her by her guardian, Aunt Nuala. Not that Roisin held it against her aunt, who had risked her own life to save Roisin when the *Gestapo* had almost captured her in Cork in the early days of the occupation.

Back then she had gone under her real name of Rachel Clarke, and it was Aunt Nuala who had created her new identity of Roisin Tierney. Aunt Nuala – Mrs Tierney to the other staff in work – was a civil servant in the registration office in Dublin's Custom House. As a childless widow she had gone back to work when her husband had died five years ago, and none of the neighbours in Phibsboro had questioned it when she had provided a home to the alleged niece of her deceased husband, Liam Tierney.

In fact, Rachel was the child of Nuala's wayward brother, Eddie Clarke, who had left Ireland as a young man and fallen out with most of his family when he married a Jewish Englishwoman.

Rachel owed her life to the fact that Nuala had stayed in loose contact with Eddie, and since the escape from Cork nobody in Dublin had ever uncovered Nuala's deception. With her access to official records, her aunt had created the correct paperwork to match her new identity – whereby Rachel became Roisin.

That had been two years ago, and by now she actually thought of herself as Roisin. Over the years Nuala had discreetly tried to keep tabs on Roisin's parents, and the good news was that her mother was still in a labour unit at Spike Island in County Cork. Prisoners there were worked hard and badly fed, but the important thing was that she had survived. Terrifying stories had filtered back to Ireland of Jews in Europe being murdered in huge numbers, so that Mam being kept in Spike Island was definitely the lesser of two evils. The news on her father was less clear. Nuala was able to establish that Edward Clarke had been shipped to a forced labour unit in Germany's Ruhr Valley, but that was where the trail had gone cold. Roisin refused to give up hope, however, and she prayed every night that Dad was still alive, that Mam was well in Cork, and that no one would discover her own Jewish ancestry.

Her thoughts were interrupted now as Mary turned around to her, a mischievous look in her eye. 'Hey, Roisin,' she said in a low voice, 'what do you call a Hitler Youth who's good-looking, smart, and kind?'

'What do you call him?

'One of a kind!'

Roisin liked the way Mary tried to find the fun in any situation and she laughed, as did Kevin and Dennis O'Sullivan. But Dennis indicated the Hitler Youth who was chatting now to Mr Cox.

'Don't let him hear you,' he warned.

'Pity about him,' said Mary. 'We didn't ask him to come and

35

preach to us.'

Dennis was about to respond, but Mary raised her hand. 'It's OK, I wouldn't say it loud enough for him to hear.'

'What's this?' said Roisin, seeing a piece of paper in Kevin's hand.

Kevin grinned. 'My tribute to the Hitler Youth,' he said, discreetly showing them a drawing. Kevin was a good cartoonist, and Roisin was amused to see that he had done a witty caricature of the self-important Hitler Youth.

'Brilliant!' said Mary.

'Bit smart-alecky,' said Dennis. 'I wonder what your man would say if he saw it.' Before anyone could respond, Dennis snatched the drawing.

'Give it back, Dennis. That's just between us,' said Kevin.

Dennis ignored him and quickly began folding the sheet of paper.

'What do you think you're doing?' demanded Mary.

'Making a plane,' answered Dennis, folding the drawing to turn it into a paper plane. 'If I launch it well it should reach our friend!' he said, indicating the Hitler Youth.

'No!' cried Kevin, reaching for the drawing.

Dennis easily evaded him, and Roisin felt a surge of annoyance. Why did Dennis have to turn a joke into something nasty? She knew that some boys would forcibly tackle Dennis, but Kevin wasn't aggressive by nature, and Dennis was bigger and had a more domineering personality.

'If he sees that drawing, Kevin will be in trouble,' she said quietly but firmly. 'But you'll be in trouble too for throwing it. And Mary and I will make sure he knows who threw it. Right, Mary?

'Absolutely.'

Dennis looked annoyed. 'Keep your hair on. It was only a joke.'

Roisin thought this was what bullies often said when challenged about picking on someone, and she looked Dennis in the eye. 'I've seen funnier jokes.'

'Look in the mirror and you'll see a better one!' retorted Dennis. He threw the drawing towards Kevin, and then walked away.

For a moment no one spoke, then Mary broke the ice. 'There he goes,' she said, looking after Dennis, 'three times winner of the Nicest Boy in Phibsboro!'

The others laughed, and Roisin was glad they had stood up for Kevin. But she knew she had made an enemy of Dennis O'Sullivan, and she sensed, uncomfortably, that at some stage that might be a problem.

CHAPTER THREE

The dipping sun sparkled on the waters of the Royal Canal, but the evening air had turned cool, and most of those who had been sunning themselves or strolling along the towpath had now made for home. Dennis O'Sullivan approached the Third Lock, pausing briefly to look down into the swirling waters. The lock looked dark and cold, and to his right Dennis could see the forbidding high walls of Mountjoy Jail, looming in silhouette against the sky. He suppressed a slight shiver, then moved on, trying to appear as though he hadn't a care in the world. But although he might have fooled a casual observer, inwardly he was nervous about the meeting to which he was heading.

He started down the decline towards Binns Bridge and told himself that he had little to worry about. Binns Bridge was far enough from home to make it unlikely that he would encounter friends or neighbours. But even if he met someone unexpectedly, he was good at improvising and talking his way out of things. And besides, despite a touch of nerves, another part of him liked the idea of secret meetings, and savoured the idea of putting one over on other people.

Always look out for yourself, his father said, *because no one else will.* Dennis knew that the O'Sullivan family had suffered badly during the 1913 labour lockout, when thousands of Dublin workers had been starved into submission by employers bent on breaking the trade unions. Dennis had often heard his father proclaim that the O'Sullivans would never, *ever,* be losers again.

'Why can't people just be practical and deal with the Nazis?' Da had said at dinner earlier this evening. 'They won the war, they rule Western Europe; they're the facts. It's like primitive tribes that rebelled against the Romans, when they should have been smart and accepted Roman rule.'

Dennis had thought that the Americans and the British weren't exactly primitive tribes, but he didn't argue the point with Da, who didn't like to be contradicted.

Dennis walked on now through the summer evening, slowing down as he approached Binns Bridge. There were seats along the towpath here, and he saw a broad-shouldered man sitting on the far end of the nearest seat, reading a newspaper. Dennis came to a stop and sat at the opposite end of the bench, as though resting. The man paid him no heed, but Dennis knew his arrival had been noted.

Dennis looked around casually, observing that there was an old woman at one of the other seats. Otherwise there was nobody within hearing distance, and the old woman was a good distance away and wouldn't pick up a word that was said.

'Good evening, *Kommissar,*' said Dennis politely. He knew that Germans took their titles seriously, and *Kriminalkommissar* Vogts wasn't a man with whom you behaved familiarly. Neither Dennis nor Vogts looked directly at each other, but the *Gestapo* man lowered his newspaper slightly.

'Good evening.'

Despite his German accent and clipped way of speaking, Vogts had excellent English. Dennis knew that he had served in Liverpool and Cork before being posted to Dublin, and he suspected that Vogts had had plenty of practice in both places at speaking English – and at crushing resistance to Nazi rule.

'What have you to report?'

'I checked out the fields near Finglas that you asked me about.'

'And?'

'You were right. There are fellas drilling there. But they're not very serious. Most of them only have pistols, and even those looked ancient.'

'You got close enough to see that?'

'Yes. They don't see a friendly kid as a threat. I got chatting to one of them and I found out they'll be drilling again next Thursday night at eight.'

'Excellent,' said Vogts. 'Very good work.'

Without turning around, he slid a sealed envelope along the seat, and Dennis took it unobtrusively and slipped it into his pocket. The *Gestapo* man wasn't extravagant with either praise or payment, but the money was paid regularly, and in cash, and Dennis was building up a nice nest egg.

He recalled the first encounter with Vogts. Dennis had got his nerve up and walked into Fitzgibbons Street police station and asked for the duty *Gestapo* officer. The policeman on desk duty hadn't taken him seriously, but when Dennis had insisted that he had important information he had eventually been taken to an interview room and was joined by *Kriminalkommissar* Vogts. Dennis had told him the address of a premises in Cabra where a back-street printing press was turning out anti-Nazi handbills, and that had been the start of an ongoing relationship between them.

Dennis had convinced the German that people on guard against informers would think in terms of adults, so that a kid with his eyes and ears open could regularly glean information of value.

The fate of those using the printing press had played on Dennis's mind briefly – but only briefly. As Da said, resisting the Nazis was stupid, and people should just get on with their lives. And if some people insisted on staying stupid, then the O'Sullivans wouldn't be among them. Notwithstanding that, Dennis had never told his family – or anybody else – of his role, and there was a certain thrill to be had from fooling everybody.

And now Dennis was pleased to have satisfied the spy master, who could exude a disturbing chilliness if the information provided didn't satisfy him.

'Anything else to report?' asked the German.

'No, that's all for now.'

'I have something for you to check out.'

'OK.'

'You live quite near the Botanic Gardens, yes?'

'Yes.'

'Start spending time there, but without drawing attention.'

'What am I looking out for?' asked Dennis.

'We've heard whispers – though it might be no more than rumour – that criminal elements are meeting there.'

'Criminal elements?'

'Insurrectionists. People resisting the rule of law.'

Much as Dennis admired the Germans for their vigour and their military skill, he thought it was a bit rich for the *Gestapo* to quote the rule of law. He knew better, though, than to give any hint of his thinking to Vogts and he nodded in agreement. 'Right.'

'Keep a sharp lookout, and if you see anything suspicious report back to me.'

'Fine. When do you want me to start?'

'Immediately.'

Ask a foolish question, thought Dennis. *The Nazis always wanted things their way and to their schedule.*

'Anything else you see and hear, I still want to know, understood?'

'Yes, *Kommissar.*'

'But this is your main mission for the moment.'

'I'll give it my full attention.'

'Give *every* task I set you your full attention,' said Vogts, and although he didn't look up from his newspaper, Dennis felt as though the German's eyes were boring into him.

'Of course, *Kommissar.*'

'Very well, that will be all. Good work on Finglas.'

'Thank you.' Dennis felt relieved as he always did when finished with Vogts, but he also was buoyed by the *Gestapo* man's praise. Still maintaining the fiction that he and Vogts were total strangers, he stood, felt the comforting presence of the cash in his pocket, then turned and headed for home.

CHAPTER FOUR

Kevin didn't like going behind his father's back, and he hesitated at the door to Dad's study. It was a mild May evening and Mam was downstairs giving a violin lesson, while Dad was still in town at a Corporation meeting. Dad was trusting by nature and never locked the study door, which made Kevin feel like even more of a snoop. But German rule *had* to be resisted, and Kevin needed to play a part in that, however small. Overcoming his reluctance, he stepped quietly into the back bedroom that his father had converted into a study.

He felt his pulses racing but forced himself to take a deep breath and to act calmly. He knew he wasn't physically brave, but this was his way of fighting back, and he wanted to do it well. Even so, he felt uncomfortable going through his father's papers, and he had to remind himself of why he was here. He had always disliked bullies, and the Nazis seemed to Kevin to be the most horrible bullies ever. On top of which, they provided a local outlet for Irish thugs and bullies, some of whom had eagerly – and violently - grasped their opportunity.

With the help of such people, the occupiers had tightened their grip on every aspect of Irish life in the two and a half years since the invasion. Nowadays the streets of Dublin were festooned with swastikas, and Nazis of all types – Hitler Youth, *Gestapo, Luftwaffe* and *Kriegsmarine* – were to be seen throughout the city. Even Dublin's Phoenix Park, which was once famed as the largest walled park in any capital city in Europe, was now home to the country's ruler, the *Reich Protector*, who lived in the mansion that had previously housed the President of Ireland.

And now I'm defying them, thought Kevin, as he flicked through the folders in his father's desk. He dismissed those that related to Da's auctioneering business, and sought instead any paperwork that had to do with his role as a councillor. He saw minutes of meetings and transport orders for fruit, meat, and vegetables that were being shipped to Germany. Kevin thought it was shameful that people were going hungry in Ireland while large quantities of food were being exported to feed the insatiable German army.

He opened another folder marked *Jewish Property*. Skimming the documents within, he felt a growing sense of disgust. The paperwork was a list of property and goods that had been confiscated from Irish Jews for re-distribution by the authorities. *How could you even begin to justify stealing someone's home or business simply because they were of a particular religion?* he thought. Kevin knew from his father that the Jewish community in Ireland had always been small, and there had rarely been friction between Ireland's Jews and their Christian fellow citizens. Now, however, no Irish Jews were living freely, and those who were not already dead were in concentration camps.

Kevin closed the folder and replaced it. Just having handled it made him feel unclean. In fairness to his father, Kevin knew he didn't like much of what he had to do under German orders. He had once asked why Dad didn't just resign his seat on the corporation, and stick to his work as an auctioneer. The answer had been chilling. If the Nazis interpreted his stepping down as a form of resistance, the whole family could be classified as enemies of the state, and end up executed, or in a concentration camp. So Dad continued as a councillor.

Kevin thought that one of the worst things about the Nazi occupation was how people were forced to make compromises with their consciences, just in order to survive. Kevin's own conscience wasn't entirely clear. If what he was doing now – partly to feel better about himself – were ever to come out, it would mean disaster for the family. But risk or no risk, he *had* to do something to fight back.

Kevin opened another council file, then felt a shiver go up his spine. It was a transport order allocating train carriages to ship a large number of prisoners from camps in Ireland to labour units in Germany. *Slave labour,* thought Kevin, *where people were worked to death*. He had heard the horror stories that had made their way back to Ireland.

He quickly jotted down the details from the document. *If the Resistance knew in advance, maybe they could do something to save the prisoners. Or perhaps that was wishful thinking.* Either way, Kevin knew he had stumbled upon something significant. He finished taking down the information, replaced the paperwork exactly as he had found it, and walked out of the room.

Mary thought Friday night was the best night of the week. She loved being part of Phibsboro Youth Club and rarely missed the weekly gathering. Tonight she was sitting with Roisin and Kevin and they were finishing the evening with Arts and Crafts. There was a relaxed atmosphere as each member wove coloured rope around a wooden frame to make a stool. Mr Cox had taught them how to do it, and Mary found working with her hands really satisfying.

Right now Mr Cox had left the room to take a telephone call, and the already relaxed atmosphere had become slightly boisterous.

'Here – how do you get a squirrel to like you?' cried Dennis O'Sullivan.

'I don't know,' said Mary, 'how do you get a squirrel to like you?'

'Act like a nut!' said Dennis.

Everyone laughed, and Mary was glad to see Dennis in such outgoing mood. He could be fun when he was in good humour, like tonight, and she was glad that the minor run-in they had had over Kevin's cartoon at last week's club meeting seemed to be forgotten.

'I have one,' said Roisin. 'What do you call a boomerang that won't come back?'

'What?' asked Kevin.

'A stick!'

'That's really silly,' said Dennis.

'But you're laughing, aren't you?' countered Roisin.

'Because it's so daft.'

'All right then I'll give you a clever one,' said Mary. 'What do you call a magician's dog?'

'What?' queried Dennis.

'A Labracadabrador!'

Everyone laughed, and Roisin raised her hands in mock surrender. 'Fair enough, that's a clever joke.'

'Thank you. Now it's your turn, Kevin,' said Mary, hoping to keep the fun going.

'Ah, I'm not great at telling jokes,' said Kevin.

'You don't have to be great,' said Mary. 'Go on, I promise I'll laugh, even if it's awful!'

'OK,' said Kevin with a grin. 'I do know one. 'Why was the baby strawberry crying?'

'Why *was* the baby strawberry crying?' asked Mary playfully.

'Her Mam and Dad were in a jam!'

Again everyone laughed, and Mary was pleased for Kevin. Then Dennis spoiled the atmosphere by turning to Kevin with a smirk.

'I suppose you'll be crying yourself, Burke,' he said.

'How do you mean?' asked Kevin.

'This sunny weather we're having. If your freckles keep joining up, they'll cover your whole face!'

Dennis was rewarded by a laugh from Terry Lawless and Peadar Feeney, two slightly dim boys who looked up to him. Mary could see, though, that Kevin was taken aback, and that he wasn't sure how to respond. They had been friends since starting together in Junior Infants, and Mary knew that being kind himself, Kevin wasn't good at dealing with aggression from others. She felt really disappointed that Dennis had suddenly changed the mood from fun to mean-spiritedness, but before she could say anything Roisin intervened.

'You're no one to speak, Dennis,' she said. 'Sure you've a turn in your eye.'

'What?' said Dennis angrily, turning to her.

'You've a gunner eye,' said Roisin calmly.

'I have not!' said Dennis. He turned to the boy beside him. 'I don't, sure I don't?'

Before the boy could reply Roisin responded. 'No, actually, you don't.'

'So why did you say I do?'

'So you'd know what it's like to have someone make remarks about you. Just for a second you were worried about what people would think, weren't you? And you shouldn't have to worry, and neither should Kevin, or anyone else. In the words of Father Cunningham: *Do unto others as you'd have them do unto you!*'

Roisin did a perfect imitation of the pompous local priest who sometimes did the Children's Mass that most of the club members attended on Sundays.

The others laughed at her spot-on interpretation of the priest's voice, and Mary thought it was smart of Roisin to make her point using humour. Mary could see that Dennis wasn't sure how to react, then the moment passed as Mr Cox came into the room, ringing the hand bell that signified that the club night had come to an end.

Dennis looked put out and he left with Terry and Peadar without saying anything. *Pity about him*, thought Mary, still annoyed at the needless way he had picked on Kevin.

'I just need to nip in to the toilet,' said Roisin, 'will you hang on for me?'

'Of course,' said Mary.

Roisin left them, and Mary turned to Kevin.

'Don't mind what Dennis said.'

'Having freckles doesn't bother me. But if it wasn't that, it would be something else. He just doesn't like me.'

'Well, everyone else does, so don't lose any sleep over an eejit like Dennis O'Sullivan.'

'No. Anyway, there's bigger stuff to worry about,' said Kevin, his expression serious.

'Like what?'

Kevin looked around at the other members who were preparing to leave, and at Mr Cox who was packing away the Arts and Crafts material. 'Let's find somewhere quiet,' he suggested.

'OK,' said Mary, her curiosity aroused.

They crossed to an alcove at the far end of the room, then Kevin faced her and spoke in a low voice. 'I found something in Dad's study. It's information that's got to reach the Resistance.'

'I'll make sure it does.'

'This is more urgent than the other stuff I've passed on.'

'Yes?'

'They're planning to ship prisoners out of Ireland, to work camps in Germany. *Death camps*, more like.'

'God.'

'You can read it yourself when you get home,' said Kevin, taking an envelope out of his pocket. 'But I think it sounds really bad.'

He handed over the envelope, and just as Mary took it Roisin reappeared.

'There you are!' she said. 'I didn't know where you'd gone.'

Mary quickly shoved the envelope into the pocket of her cardigan. 'Sorry, we just…we just didn't want Mr Cox listening to us,' she answered. It was a weak explanation, and she hoped she didn't sound as flustered as she felt.

'Right…' said Roisin. She looked at Mary curiously, but said nothing about the envelope.

'Will we be on our way?' said Kevin, in what Mary knew was an attempt at distraction.

'Sure,' answered Roisin.

'Grand,' said Mary with a smile. Then she made for the door with her friends, anxious to read the contents of the envelope, and hoping that Roisin would be too polite to question what had just taken place.

'A little treat, girls!' said Aunt Nuala with a flourish as she placed a packet of sweets on the table. Roisin and Mary were in the sunlit kitchen of Nuala's house in Shandon Park, and late May sunshine beamed in the window and warmed the room.

'Thanks very much!' said Roisin.

'Yes, thanks, Mrs Tierney,' said Mary appreciatively.

Mary lived three doors up the road, and Roisin had invited her down to play gramophone records, as Aunt Nuala was going out for her regular Saturday night in town. Most Saturdays Aunt Nuala met her unmarried friend Ita, and they went to the theatre or one of the many city centre cinemas. But although Roisin was twelve now, her aunt didn't like leaving her in the house alone, and so Mary had agreed to keep her company.

'Don't eat them all and make yourselves sick,' said Nuala, indicating the sweets.

'As if we would!' answered Mary playfully.

'How do I look?' asked Nuala, giving a tiny twirl.

Mary nodded enthusiastically. 'Smashing, Mrs T.'

'Yes, very smart,' agreed Roisin. She looked approvingly at Aunt Nuala, knowing that she took a pride in her appearance. Clothing was strictly rationed, with coupons having to be provided for any major item, and many people's clothes had become worn-looking. Nuala, however, was an excellent needlewoman and was always well turned out. Although she was old – Roisin knew that she was forty-one – she was attractive, with wavy brown hair and sparkling eyes, and Roisin was relieved that she hadn't been snapped up by some eligible man in the five years that she had been a widow.

It wasn't that she would begrudge her aunt some happiness;

Roisin really loved her. But if Nuala married again, questions might arise about Roisin's own background. The Jewish link had to be kept hidden at all costs, and both Nuala and Roisin had been cautious in the extreme since Roisin's flight to Dublin over two years previously. Luckily Roisin had never had a strong Cork accent, and she had quickly adopted the middle-of-the-road Dublin accent of her friends and neighbours. She had worked hard too at memorising the backstory that Nuala had made up for her, until it had become second nature to think of herself as Roisin Tierney rather than Rachel Clarke.

Now her aunt waved farewell, and the two girls were left alone. Roisin felt nervous. She had wanted an opportunity to raise a tricky topic with her friend, but now that they were on their own she wasn't sure how to start. She handed Mary a sweet and took one herself, then before she could figure out what to say, Mary spoke. 'So, what's the new record you got?'

'Well…it's not really new. Aunt Nuala got it second-hand. It's called "Blues in the Night".'

'I don't think I know it.'

'I'd say you'll like it. Will we go into the parlour and put it on?' said Roisin.

'Sure.'

Roisin took up the bag of sweets, and they crossed the hall and entered the parlour, where Mary sat on the sofa, while Roisin took the record from its sleeve. She placed it on the gramophone turntable and lowered the needle. For a few seconds there was hiss and cackle, then the smooth sound of a trumpet filled the air.

'Gosh. I like the sound of this already!' said Mary.

'Yes, it's great,' answered Roisin, then she tried to figure out what to say while her friend listened to the music.

'Brilliant piece,' said Mary when the last notes faded away. 'Full marks to your aunt for buying that.'

'Yes.'

'So, what will we play next?'

'Before we do,' said Roisin, 'can I … can I ask you something?'

'Of course.'

'It's to do with Kevin.'

'What about Kevin?'

'Well, when I came back from the toilet last night, I felt…I felt like I was interrupting something.'

Mary looked uneasy, but now that Roisin had started she had to see this through. 'I saw him giving you a note and just wondered if…if maybe he wants to be your boyfriend?'

'No!'

'No?'

'Definitely not!'

Mary's response had been instant and emphatic, and Roisin felt relieved that their circle of friends wasn't going to be complicated, as she had feared it might. She hoped her relief wasn't too obvious, and she quickly continued. 'Not that there's anything wrong with Kevin – he's great. And if he *was* your boyfriend, that would be–'

'Roisin!' said Mary, raising a hand and cutting her short. 'He's not my boyfriend. He's a really good friend who happens to be a boy.'

'Right.'

'We were just chatting, and you took us by surprise,' explained Mary.

Roisin sensed that there was more to it than that, and she thought it strange that Mary was making no mention of the letter that she had taken from Kevin. Roisin's instinct was not to pry, but another part of her thought that she had come this far, and they may as well get everything out in the open.

'It's just that I saw him give you a note. And then there seemed to be…I don't know…'

Mary hesitated, then spoke reassuringly. 'That was just a letter for my mother. I give you my word, Roisin. Kevin isn't trying to be my boyfriend, and I'm not trying to be his girlfriend.'

'Fine.'

'So, what's the next record?'

'Eh…will I play "Tea for Two"?'

'Oh, yes, I love that.'

Roisin removed 'Blues in the Night' and replaced it with the new record, but her mind was racing. Maybe Mary's explanation was all there was to it, and perhaps she had been reading too much into a minor incident. *And yet.* They had looked slightly guilty when she interrupted them last night. And if Kevin had a letter for Mary's mother, why didn't he stick it in her letterbox twenty yards from his hall door, instead of bringing it to the youth club? But if she questioned Mary any further it would be like calling her a liar. *Better to leave it for now*, thought Roisin. *Don't make a mountain of a molehill.*

The music began to play, and she sat back, smiled at her friend, and hoped she hadn't created an awkwardness between them.

CHAPTER FIVE

Dennis loved the sweet juicy taste of the tinned peaches his mother had served for desert. He held the fruit in his mouth for a moment, savouring its delicious flavour and texture. Part of his pleasure came from knowing that few people in Dublin could enjoy the luxury of tinned fruit. Since the start of the war there had been rationing, and items like tinned peaches usually had to be obtained on the black market.

Father Cunningham had talked about Eve eating forbidden fruit in the Garden of Eden during one of his laborious sermons at Mass, and Dennis was amused now, to think that he too was eating forbidden fruit.

As his father said, though, what was the point of a family working hard if they couldn't reward themselves? As the youngest of six children Dennis had two brothers and a sister who had left home and emigrated before the wartime restraints on travel that the Nazis had imposed. But Anne and Frances, his other sisters, worked in shops in town and still lived with the family. It meant that with Da also earning a wage as a foreman in a printing works, they had three regular wage packets coming in. And as his father said, it wasn't the O'Sullivans' fault that there were food shortages – so why shouldn't they get their hands on as much as they could?

Dennis would have liked to boast about the money he was

earning from *Kriminalkommissar* Vogts, but his instincts told him to keep secret his work as a collaborator. It wasn't that his family disapproved of the Nazis. Da said that in any situation you had to recognise who had the power, and do a deal with whoever that was. And despite some serious setbacks in the war on the Russian Front, the Nazis were still firmly in control as the occupying power in Western Europe. So the O'Sullivans wouldn't waste time and energy objecting to German rule, but would instead do whatever they could to get ahead themselves.

Sunday dinner was drawing to a close now – there were never second helpings of treats like canned peaches – and Dennis asked to be excused. Da was already undoing the top button of his trousers and would soon be falling asleep in his armchair with the Sunday paper slipping from his grasp. Anne and Frances were meeting friends, and Ma was about to bake a rhubarb tart, so there was no objection when he thanked his mother for the meal and stepped away from the table.

'Where are you off to, Den?' asked his father as he prepared to leave.

'Just going to play football with some of the lads,' he replied, the lie coming easily. In fact he was due to report to Vogts. The *Gestapo* man rarely met him in the same place twice, and this afternoon their rendezvous was in a quiet corner of Glasnevin Cemetery

'Make sure you're back in time for tea,' said his mother.

'I will,' he answered, then he made for the hall door and stepped out into Leinster Street, the red bricked terraced houses bathed in bright May sunshine.

Dennis headed for Phibsboro Road and his mood changed from relaxation to one of alertness. Meeting Vogts was always a little nerve-wracking, and the German had the knack of keeping Dennis slightly off balance. It was worth it, though, to be in league with such a powerful figure. In the uncertainty of occupation who could tell when a favour might be needed in dealing with the authorities? And if that day ever came, being an ally of *Kriminal-kommissar* Vogts would be a very strong card to play.

Meanwhile, Dennis would keep saving his payments from the *Gestapo* officer with the goal of buying a motorbike when he was old enough to get a licence. There would, of course, be no readily available petrol for civilian motorbikes or cars until the war was over. But the war would end one day, and when it did he would be ready. He loved anything to do with engines, and was attending his first year of technical school with the intention of being apprenticed as a mechanic.

First, though, he had to satisfy his handler. He had no progress to report regarding suspicious activity in the Botanic Gardens. But he would emphasise how much time and effort he had put into keeping the place under discreet observation, and how he was willing to continue it, if necessary. And several youths involved with the Resistance had been arrested in the area he had described north of Finglas, so he knew that that would stand to his credit. All in all things were going nicely, and he strode on through the early summer sunshine, eager for another payday, and to hear what mission Vogts might offer him next.

Kevin felt a tug on his fishing line and he excitedly began to reel in his catch. He loved the tranquility of fishing almost as much as the thrill of feeling a fish bite, and even though the canal bank wasn't far from his house in Shandon Park, it was peaceful here, especially on balmy nights like tonight.

He landed the fish, pleased to see that it was a fair-sized trout. Although his father's role as a councillor provided the Burkes with precious petrol coupons and enabled them to get superior rations, there was still satisfaction to be had from bringing home fresh fish that his mother could cook. Dad was the main bread-winner, while Mam also brought in an income with her violin lessons, but Kevin liked the idea of contributing too. He re-baited his hook and cast off again, then looked up as a familiar figure approached.

'Mary,' he said in greeting.

'Are they biting?' she asked.

'Got one trout so far.'

'That's not bad.'

'Yes, it was a decent one. What has you up here?'

'I was looking for you.'

'Oh?'

'I called in for you, but your dad said you were here.'

Kevin thought there was a seriousness about Mary's manner

and he looked at her enquiringly. 'Is everything OK?'

'Yes, but I need to talk. Can we sit down for a minute?' she asked, indicating the thick bough of a felled tree nearby.

'Sure,' said Kevin. He wedged his fishing rod between a couple of rocks, then crossed to the tree and sat beside his friend.

'I eh…I have a suggestion,' she said.

'Yes?'

'But you're probably not going to like it.'

'What is it?'

'You know the information you gave me about the train shipping the prisoners? I'm meeting my father tomorrow night to pass it on.'

'Good.'

'But Roisin picked up that something was going on, on Friday night. She asked me about it.'

Kevin felt a twinge of unease. 'What did you tell her?'

'That you'd given me a letter from your mother.'

'Right. And did she believe you?'

'I'm not sure.'

'So…what's your suggestion?'

Mary hesitated briefly, then looked him in the eye. 'I think maybe we should swear her to secrecy, but bring her in on what we're doing.'

'Are you mad?!'

'She hates the Nazis. She'd be completely on our side.'

'That's not the point,' said Kevin, shocked at his friend's

proposal.

'How is it not the point?'

'Because you can be sympathetic and still let something slip. Nobody knows who's a spy or an informer, so one slip could mean disaster.'

'I know that, Kevin.'

'Then think it through. One mistake, one careless word and that's it. For you, me, our families.'

'Yes, but...'

'Mary! We're up against murderers. People who shot union leaders dead just for calling a strike!'

'Do you think I haven't thought about that? Every single day since this started? I haven't been able to meet Dad openly for over two years. I know the stakes, Kevin.'

'Yes. Sorry...I just...'

'It's all right. I understand we've to be really careful. But Roisin is a really good friend to both of us. And it's going to get harder and harder to keep misleading her. Do you want to lose her as a friend?'

'No, of course not.'

'If we keep lying to her, it's going to come between us.'

Kevin recognised that this was true. He already felt uncomfortable whenever he and Mary made excuses to meet up behind Roisin's back, even though the Resistance work that they were doing was important.

'The other thing is she's really smart,' continued Mary. 'The time might come when we need help. And she'd be brilliant to have on the team.'

Kevin reflected a moment, and then looked at his friend. 'There's one thing that you haven't thought about.'

'What's that?'

'Maybe she wouldn't thank us for getting her involved.'

'I'd never try and *force* her into anything. But we should give her the choice.'

'Except that telling her that *we're* involved could be a problem. If she knows we're breaking the law and she says nothing, that's a crime in itself, according to the Nazis.'

'I honestly don't think that would bother her.'

'Maybe,' conceded Kevin. 'But we can't be sure.'

'There's only one way to find out.'

Kevin hesitated. 'Your father might have a problem with another person being taken into the circle.'

'He's left us to fend for ourselves. I don't mean that in a bad way – he's made huge sacrifices,' said Mary. 'But Mam and I had to get used to doing things for ourselves. And that includes making decisions. So if I feel it's right to trust Roisin, then I can make that decision.'

Kevin nodded. 'Right.'

'So what do you think?'

Kevin grimaced. 'I'm torn. It would be great never to tell Roisin another lie. But I'm nervous too. I don't know if it's better to be over-cautious, or if I'm being too timid.'

'I think we should tell her, Kevin. But this affects you as much as me. So unless we both agree, I won't do anything.'

Kevin looked away, his gaze drifting across the still waters of the canal. He knew he could go round in circles, forever debating the pros and cons. *Better to go with his gut instinct.* He turned back to Mary.

'OK,' he said. 'Let's tell her.'

'Sure?'

'No, not absolutely,' he answered. 'But if I waited till I was certain about everything, I'd never do anything.'

Mary nodded. 'So we tell her.'

'Yes.'

'When will we do it?'

'Maybe now, before I lose my nerve?' said Kevin. 'My mind won't be on the fishing after this, so why don't I pack up and we'll go tell her together?'

'Great,' said Mary.

'All right then. Let's do it.'

CHAPTER SIX

'**G**od almighty! We have to stop this…' said Commandant Flanagan.

Mary stood with her father at their rendezvous spot in Glasnevin Cemetery, the evening sun starting to dip. There was nobody else around, and the scent of wild roses hung in the evening air. But despite the isolated location, face-to-face encounters were a risk, though Mary felt justified now in having sought a meeting.

They had a system whereby she could make contact by marking a stone on the canal bank that was regularly checked by one of Commandant Flanagan's Resistance agents. Mary had indicated that she had urgent information to pass on, and she was gratified that her father shared her view on its importance.

He read through Kevin's hand-written note again, then looked at Mary. 'That train has to be stopped,' he said.

'How can you do that?'

'I don't know. But we'll have to find a way.'

'Kevin said he thought the place in Germany where they're sending the prisoners, that…that it might be a death camp.'

Commandant Flanagan nodded grimly. 'He's right. None of the camps treat prisoners well, but some of them deliberately work them to death.'

'That's awful, Dad.'

'Pretty much *everything* the Nazis do is awful.'

Mary knew that this was true, yet she felt a sense of relief now that she had shared the burden of information with her father. The night before last it had been a big relief too when she and Kevin had come clean to Roisin about their activity with the Resistance. *No need to tell Da about that*, she thought, knowing his obsession with security. Besides, they had sworn Roisin to absolute secrecy, and she had thanked them for trusting her so much.

It was over two years since the Nazis had defeated the Irish army and her father had gone underground – two years of deceit, and fear of betrayal, and always having to be on her guard. Not that she was the only one suffering. People all over Ireland had been shot, beaten and tortured by the *Gestapo*, and outspoken journalists, priests, and politicians had been rounded up in the early days of the occupation and never seen again. Mam only saw Dad about twice a year when the family went on holidays to Mam's brother's farm in Laois, where Dad could visit in the dead of night from the Resistance camps in the Slieve Bloom Mountains. And even then it wasn't safe for Mary's younger siblings to know that their father was still alive, which meant that Dad had to forgo seeing his own children.

'We're going to have to come out of the shadows,' said Dad, interrupting her musings. 'We'll have to mount a big operation.'

'Yes?'

'It's one thing blowing up bridges and disrupting Nazi supply lines. But we've got to really take on the Germans from time to time. This is one of those times.'

'That sounds dangerous.'

'Can't be helped. Some of the prisoners will be Irish Jews – the ones who survived so far. But a lot of them will be Irish soldiers who fought on and were captured. We owe it to both groups to try and save them.'

'There'll be a price, though, won't there?' said Mary. 'If German soldiers are killed, there'll be reprisals. Really bad ones.'

Her father said nothing, and she pressed him. 'Won't there, Dad?'

He held her gaze and nodded. 'Yes. It's a horrible choice. We know they'll murder innocent civilians. But if we don't fight back at all, there's no point having a Resistance. And having a Resistance ties down German troops – troops that would otherwise be free to fight on the Eastern Front.'

Mary knew this was important. Fierce and bloody battles were being fought between the Nazis and the Red Army in Russia. According to rumours, the Russians were getting the upper hand, and every German division pinned down here in Ireland would help. So until the British, Americans, Canadians and Free French could launch an invasion to start a Western Front, resistance had to continue.

'Is there enough time to come up with a plan between now and next Monday?' asked Mary.

'There'll have to be. Though six days isn't much to pull off something this big.'

'I want to help, Dad.' Mary saw that her father was about to protest but she raised a hand to stop him. 'Please. There's no point telling me it's dangerous. *Everything* to do with our lives is dangerous. But kids can be useful; the Germans don't see us as a threat. So if there's any way that I can help, I want to.'

Her father didn't reply, and Mary decided to push on. 'When we're free again one day, Dad, I want to look back and say I did more than deliver messages. Hundreds of men's lives could be saved next week. I really want to help make that happen.'

Mary sensed that this was one of the rare occasions when her father didn't know what to say, and she looked him full in the eye. 'You've done what *you* feel is right, Dad. Please, let *me* do the same. Let me play my part.'

Roisin cycled up Prospect Road, her head in a swirl. She was heading for an arranged meeting with Kevin and Mary and she tried to get her thoughts in order as she pedalled along. Monday night's revelation that her friends were involved with the Resistance had shocked her. Looking back though, it made sense that Mary would follow in Commandant Flanagan's footsteps, and that someone with Kevin's sense of justice would take the opposite stance to his collaborating father.

Roisin had felt honoured that Kevin and Mary trusted her with their secret; in effect putting their lives in her hands. It made her feel deceitful though about not revealing her own big secret. But keeping her Jewish background hidden had been a matter of life and death, with many Jews having died at the hands of the Nazis, and instinctively she had held back, and not told of how Aunt Nuala had created her present identity.

Now she had decided that the burden of secrecy was too much to bear, and she wanted to be honest with her friends. She knew that Nuala would be horrified at the thought. It wasn't that her aunt was timid – as a girl in Mayo she had encountered the dreaded Black and Tans during the War of Independence – but Nuala was obsessed with security. *Then again, her aunt didn't need to know.* Though that too would be another secret to have to keep, and Roisin wished that life could be simpler.

She had had a sobering conversation with Nuala before leaving the house, with her aunt having managed to confirm that Roisin's mother was still in the camp on Spike Island. The government records that Aunt Nuala had access to in her civil service job didn't refer to the health or welfare of the camp's residents, but at least Roisin could console herself that her mother was definitely still alive. She wished she could send Mam a Red Cross parcel to make her life a little better, but that would be impossible without drawing attention to herself and Aunt Nuala. Still, as long as Mam was in Spike Island she was in less danger than if she got shipped to a camp in Europe.

The fate of her father, however, was still uncertain, as Nuala couldn't access the records of prisoners shipped out of the country. The one reassuring fact that Roisin clung on to was that Dad had been sent to a factory in the Ruhr Valley as part of a forced labour battalion, which was better than being sent to the kind of camp where Russian prisoners of war were deliberately starved while being worked to death.

Now, though, Roisin sat back in the saddle and freewheeled down Botanic Road, wondering how her friends would respond when they learned that her real name was Rachel Clarke, and that Roisin Tierney was an invention of her aunt's. A carefully-constructed invention, with a convincing backstory and paperwork to match – but still a fraud. *And on her mother's side she was Jewish.*

That was the part that made revealing her secret unpredictable. She knew that Mary and Kevin were good friends who were loyal and decent. But even people who were fine in most respects sometimes had a blind spot. And the Nazis had stirred up so much hatred against the Jews that it was easy for people to give way to prejudice. She had seen horrible anti-Jewish graffiti, and some Irish people had looted and vandalised Jewish homes on the South Circular Road, whose owners had fled or been arrested at the start of the Occupation.

Before she could worry about it any further, she reached the gates of the Botanic Gardens and dismounted from her bicycle. She leaned it against a lamp post, locked it, and then walked through the main entrance to the gardens. The scent of flowers carried on the breeze, and Roisin savoured the sweet bouquet even as she nervously made for the agreed meeting point where the Tolka River acted as a boundary to the Botanic Gardens.

She knew she was being super-cautious and that she could have met Mary and Kevin back at Shandon Park. For sharing her darkest secret, however, she wanted someplace where they could talk privately without fear of interruption. And as Mary and Kevin attended piano lessons on Wednesday evenings at a music school on nearby Glasnevin Hill – Kevin refused to take violin lessons from his own mother – the Botanic Gardens seemed ideal.

Roisin made her way to the river walk, then waved as she saw Kevin and Mary waiting for her by the banks of the Tolka. 'How were the music lessons?' she asked.

'Grand,' said Mary

'Boring,' said Kevin almost exactly at the same time.

Everyone laughed, then Kevin looked enquiringly at Roisin. 'So, what's this mystery meeting about?'

Roisin's smile faded, and she took a breath. 'Why don't we sit down?' she said indicating a bench at the edge of the river path. 'I've got…I've got something I want to tell you.'

Dennis made a tiny adjustment to his binoculars, wanting to make the focus perfect. There was something really satisfying about watching other people closely, he thought, while remaining unseen himself. He had always been agile and daring enough to climb to the top of tall trees, and from his current vantage point high up in a huge old oak he had a superb view of the landscape below him. The tree's heavy summer foliage and the height of his perch meant that he was all but invisible, and he had made his ascent of the oak when there had been no-one around to see him. He imagined that this must be what it was like to be a sniper, outsmarting the enemy and striking when the moment was right.

He had spent a lot of time in the Botanic Gardens lately, but so far he hadn't seen any suspicious activity that he could report back to *Kriminalkommissar*Vogts. Now, however, he was intrigued to see Mary Flanagan, Kevin Burke and Roisin Tierney engaged in what seemed like a deep conversation. He had the binoculars focussed on Roisin's face, and she was talking with great seriousness.

What were they up to? It looked like a deliberate rendezvous.Yet the three people involved lived within yards of each other. Why come to the Botanics when they could have chatted at Shandon Park? Dennis had been disappointed not to have spotted anything resembling Resistance activity, despite patient observation. But Goody-Two-Shoes Burke and his pals were up to something, and Dennis was fascinated.

It didn't occur to him that it was anything to do with the Resistance – Kevin's father worked with the Germans – but *something* was going on. Dennis moved the binoculars, flitting between Roisin, and Kevin and Mary. Part of him would love to appear suddenly and see how they responded. But that would be stupid and would show his hand.

No, he decided, far better to get Kevin when he was on his own. Then he could force some answers out of him. Pleased with his decision, he stayed unmoving in the tree, his binoculars trained on his unsuspecting neighbours.

CHAPTER SEVEN

Kevin felt uneasy. He was sitting at the kitchen table with his parents and he had just finished his favourite desert, his mother's home-made apple dumpling. Normally he would polish off a double helping without a second thought, but tonight he was conscious of the family's privilege in getting the superior rations that enabled Mam to bake it. He loved his mother, who was instinctively kind and gentle, yet part of him couldn't help but be critical of her too. She never challenged his father's dealings with the Nazis, never questioned the fact that they were doing better than so many other people. How could she simply ignore anything that was awkward and behave as if all was normal?

Since yesterday in the Botanics when Roisin had revealed her secret about being Jewish, he had grown even more uncomfortable with his father's collaboration. He understood that Dad was in a difficult position, but Roisin had given an urgency to his concerns about how Irish Jews were being treated.

'Can I...can I ask you a question, Dad?' he said now.

'Of course,' answered his father, his tone sympathetic. 'What's on your mind?'

'Is it true that if you're Jewish, they can just take away your business, or your property – and that's legal?'

Kevin could see that Dad looked troubled, but instead of

answering the question he asked one of his own. 'What's brought this on, son? Who have you been talking to?'

Kevin didn't like lying, but he had to protect Roisin. 'Eh, just some boys in school,' he answered.

'They need to be careful what they say,' said his father.

'And so do you, Kevin, if you're talking to them,' added his mother concernedly.

'It's true then?' persisted Kevin.

'After the occupation normal Irish law was suspended,' explained his father. 'So it's out of our hands, even if we mightn't like some of the things that are happening.'

'*Mightn't like?*

'It's difficult, I admit.'

'It's awful, Dad. Taking someone's home or their job, because they're a certain race…'

'It's not what we'd choose, Kevin,' said Mam. 'But what can we do?'

'We're an occupied country, son, we don't have control any more,' said his father. 'I know you struggle with that. Most Irish people do. But we have to just muddle through as best we can.'

'Try not to think too much about things you can't control, love,' said Mam. 'You'll only upset yourself.'

'And be really careful who you talk to in school. No one gets away with crossing the Nazis – whatever their age. Do you understand?'

Kevin recognised that there was no point arguing any further.

'Yes, I …I understand,' he said. He turned to his mother. 'Can I be excused please?'

'Yes, but don't forget to say your grace after meals.'

Kevin quickly blessed himself and said the prayer, then left the table.

His mind was troubled, and he collected his fishing gear, thinking that a spell at the water would help him to get his thoughts in order.

He stepped out onto Shandon Park. The June evening was still pleasantly warm, and as he made for the nearby Royal Canal he caught the scent of sweet pea from a neighbouring garden. Just as he reached the end of the street and turned the corner he heard footsteps behind him. Glancing around, he was surprised to see Dennis O'Sullivan moving briskly towards him. Something about the bigger boy's demeanour made Kevin feel on edge, but he nodded in greeting. 'Dennis.'

'Burke, the very boy I wanted.'

Dennis had said it with a sneer, and Kevin suddenly felt on guard. Although they hadn't yet reached the canal bank, they were out of sight of the houses on Shandon Park.

'Yes?' said Kevin, trying to keep his tone sounding relaxed.

'Stop for a minute. We need to talk.'

Kevin wanted to get away, but Dennis was heavier and stronger and Kevin didn't want to challenge him by refusing to talk. He stopped and lowered his fishing bag.

'What do we need to talk about?' he asked, taking care not to sound aggressive, but also trying not to sound frightened.

'Your little get-together in the Botanics,' answered Dennis.

'What get-together?'

'With Mary Flanagan and Roisin Tierney. It looked very cosy.'

Kevin realised that Dennis was referring to the meeting at which Roisin had revealed her secret. But there had been nobody around when they had spoken. How on earth had Dennis seen them?

'What…what are you talking about?' he asked, playing for time.

'Well isn't that funny?' said Dennis with a smirk. 'That's just what I was going to ask you. What were *you* talking about?'

'We were…we were just chit-chatting.'

Dennis's face hardened. 'Don't lie if you know what's good for you. You were in deep conversation. So spill the beans.'

Kevin wanted to tell Dennis to mind his own business, but he knew the bigger boy had a vicious streak and that he couldn't afford to provoke him. Kevin could feel his heart thumping but he tried to keep his voice steady.

'I don't know why you're so interested, but we were talking about Roisin's aunt being sick. The doctor told her she has asthma.' This was pure fiction, but Kevin was determined to divert Dennis from the actual conversation about Roisin's Jewish background.

Dennis looked him in the eye, and he couldn't tell whether or not he had convinced him.

'Asthma?' said Dennis. 'That must be tough.'

'Yes, it is.'

'But there's worse than asthma, isn't there? More painful things. Like having your arm broken.'

'What?'

Before Kevin knew what was happening, Dennis moved behind him and kneed him in the back. Kevin cried out, dropping his fishing rod as Dennis grabbed him by the neck while twisting his arm behind his back.

Kevin felt a searing pain as his arm was wrenched upwards, then Dennis's voice was in his ear.

'Don't treat me like a fool, Burke! Now tell me what you were talking about!'

Kevin felt an agonising pain from his arm, but he couldn't betray Roisin. 'You'll break my arm!' he cried.

'That's right. But I'll claim it was an accident, that we were just messing.'

'Please!'

'Start talking!'

Kevin felt tears of pain forming in his eyes, but he gritted his teeth. He could never beat Dennis in a fight. But there was one way he might defeat him. If he could take all the pain that Dennis inflicted, but refuse to betray his friend, then that would be a victory over the bully. A painful victory, but still a victory. *If he could hold out.*

'I said start talking!'

'No!'

Kevin felt an agonising jolt of pain as Dennis twisted his arm further.

'Talk!'

'No!'

'I *will* break your arm. Don't think I won't!'

'Then break it! And my father will have you arrested!' Kevin's arm throbbed with pain, but Dennis didn't twist it any further, and Kevin prayed that the threat of his influential father might have given the other boy pause for thought. *But if not, was he willing to have his arm broken?* He had to be – revealing Roisin's Jewish background could be a death sentence for her. He gritted his teeth determined to withstand whatever pain he had to; then suddenly he heard a loud female voice.

'Pick on someone your own size, Dennis O'Sullivan!'

To Kevin's huge relief, he felt the pressure being released on his arm, and he swung round to see that his rescuer was Mrs Maguire, a no-nonsense neighbour who lived on the far side of his road.

'We were only messing,' said Dennis. 'Just trick-acting.'

'I'll give you trick-acting,' said Mrs Maguire. 'Be off home with you now before I give you a clip on the ear. Go on!'

Dennis hesitated briefly, in what Kevin recognised as an attempt to appear uncowed, and then he walked away with a slightly sheepish air.

'Are you all right, Kevin?'

Kevin's arm throbbed painfully, but he nodded in gratitude. 'Yes, I'm OK. Thank you, Mrs Maguire.'

'Don't mind that pup,' she said, indicating the retreating Dennis.

'All the O'Sullivans were bullies, and signs-on, nobody likes them.'

'Right.'

'Come on. I'll walk with you to the canal. I'm out for a stroll.'

'Grand,' said Kevin. He picked up his fishing rod and fell into step beside his neighbour. Mrs Maguire chatted about the weather, and the latest film in the Bohemian Cinema, and Kevin chatted along. But behind it his mind was racing. How had Dennis been observing them? And how did he know they were discussing something significant? And underlying it all was a burning anger at what Dennis had subjected him to. Up to now Kevin had been at pains to avoid making an enemy of Dennis. But it was no good trying to appease a bully. And tonight something had changed. Tonight Dennis had made an enemy of *him*. He didn't know how it would all play out, but he was determined, that somehow or other Dennis O'Sullivan had to get his comeuppance. Consoled by the thought, he walked on through the warm summer evening.

'What's brown, hairy, and wears sunglasses?' asked Roisin.

Mary looked up from the stool she was making at Arts and Crafts in the youth club. 'I haven't a clue,' she said, smiling in anticipation of the answer.

'A coconut on holidays!' said Roisin.

There was laughter from the other club members seated nearby, and Mary gave her friend a thumbs up. It was good to see Roisin so relaxed, and Mary reckoned that revealing her secret Jewish background had been good for her. Mary had been shocked at first by the revelation, but then things began to make sense. Roisin had always been a bit vague about her background, and had rarely spoken of how she came to be living with her Aunt Nuala. Now Mary understood why. Having to be always on guard about her own father's secret life, she appreciated the pressure that Roisin must have been under. Her friend's strong sense of fairness also made more sense now, in light of the massively unfair way that Jews in Ireland – and across occupied Europe – were being treated.

'Boys and girls, your attention, please,' said the club organiser, Mr Cox. 'I have some good news.'

'Dennis O'Sullivan's won a one-way ticket to China!' whispered Kevin.

Mary giggled but tried not to let Mr Cox see her amusement. It was good, she thought, that Kevin could joke about the bully, though Mary and Roisin had both been disgusted when Kevin had told them about his run-in with Dennis the previous night. And although Dennis hadn't overheard the conversation in the Botanics, the fact that he had somehow observed them was still disturbing.

'Our summer camp in July has got the go-ahead,' said Mr Cox. '*Kriminalkommissar* Vogts, the German officer with responsibility for this area, has granted travel permission for our camping trip to County Galway.'

Mary could feel her hackles rising at the idea of needing Nazi approval to travel in her own country.

'He's all heart,' whispered Roisin sarcastically.

Mary responded with a quick grin, despite her annoyance that the *Gestapo's* control even extended to the operation of youth clubs. Still, it was good news that the camp was going ahead.

'We'll be spending a full week near Clifden,' continued Mr Cox. 'So keep saving, and don't raid your piggy-banks between now and then!'

'I haven't had a piggy-bank since I was seven,' said Kevin.

'Still, you know what he means,' said Mary.

'Yes, it's something to look forward to,' agreed Roisin.

Mr Cox looked around the room. 'I've another announcement before we take our break.'

'We're having a collection toward Dennis's one-way ticket!' whispered Kevin.

'*Kriminalkommissar* Vogts wishes to remind our members of the role of youth in ensuring their parents obey all *Reich* regulations,' said Mr Cox, a hint of reluctance in his tone.

'He knows what he can do with his reminder!' whispered Roisin angrily.

'And there will be a short talk at next week's meeting. A member of the Hitler Youth will tell us of his experiences at their recent rally in Cork.'

This announcement was met with a silence that pleased Mary. Everyone knew that it was dangerous to show open disrespect to the Nazis – there were too many informers around – but the club members could refuse to show enthusiasm, as was happening now.

'All right, ten-minute break,' called out Mr Cox.

'Let's go outside for a minute, I've something to tell you,' suggested Mary.

Kevin and Roisin nodded in agreement, then they made for the door.

It was a mild June evening, and some of the other club members had also stepped out, but Mary and her friends picked a spot far enough away to be able to speak privately.

'Well?' said Roisin.

'It's about the Resistance, and the train carrying the prisoners,' answered Mary. 'I couldn't tell you on the way to the club when Maisie Donnelly tagged along.'

'So what are they going to do?' asked Kevin.

'This is absolutely top secret, right?'

Roisin nodded. 'Of course.'

'They're mounting a rescue,' said Mary. 'It'll be one of the biggest blows struck since the official surrender.'

'They're going to free the prisoners?' said Kevin, unable to keep the excitement from his voice.

'Yes. There…there may be casualties but the prisoners will probably die if they're shipped to Germany. So whatever number they can free, they're lives saved.'

'God,' said Roisin. 'Attacking a train…that's…that's really dangerous.'

Mary found her stomach tightening at the thought of her

own role. But that had to be kept from her friends or they would want to be involved. And whatever about risking her own life she couldn't take the responsibility of endangering Kevin and Roisin. 'It *is* dangerous. But as Dad said, if we let them send hundreds of Irishmen to their deaths and don't lift a finger, what's the point having the Resistance?'

'True,' said Roisin.

'But there'll be reprisals for sure,' said Kevin. 'I mean, this can't be done without some Germans being killed, can it?'

'I suppose not,' answered Mary. 'But it's not our fault if the Nazis murder people afterwards. And either way Irish people will die. At least this way we can try to save more than get shot in reprisals.'

'Is there anything we can do to help?' asked Roisin.

Mary shook her head. 'No, it's all in hand. We've played our part passing on the information.' She felt bad at misleading her friends about the fact that she *would* be playing a role. But sometimes the less that people knew, the better.

'Where will they try to rescue them?' asked Kevin.

Mary hesitated. Her father's rule of thumb was that only those who *had* to know the details of an operation should be given those details. But Kevin and Roisin were completely trustworthy, and if it wasn't for Kevin they would never have known the details of the prisoner transfer. 'Liffey Junction.' Mary answered. 'They plan to make the train stop there late on Monday night.'

'Three days away,' said Roisin. 'That'll be a nerve-wracking three days.'

If only you knew, thought Mary. 'Yes,' she said aloud, trying not to let the depth of her fear show. 'Nerve-wracking is right…'

CHAPTER EIGHT

Roisin loved listening to the radio. Everything transmitted on the Irish national broadcaster, *Radio Eireann*, was strictly censored by the Nazis – as was also the case with BBC radio in occupied Britain – so Roisin rarely listened to either of those any more. Instead she and Aunt Nuala defied the Germans by listening to broadcasts on *Radio Freedom*, which was run by the Allies and transmitted from Iceland. It was strictly illegal to tune in, and anyone caught doing so was arrested, yet thousands of Irish people kept their spirits up by listening to the mixture of music and news that the station broadcast.

Tonight Roisin and her aunt had just heard that French leader, General de Gaulle, had infuriated the Nazis by setting up a provisional Free French government-in-exile. She had also heard that the US Navy was winning the war against the Japanese in the Pacific, and that the Red Army was gaining the upper hand in Russia, after the first major German defeat at the battle of Stalingrad a few months previously. It would still take an enormous effort for the Allies to launch an invasion from their bases in Iceland, but at least people had some hope that Nazi occupation wouldn't go on indefinitely.

The catchy opening bars of 'In the Mood' by the Glenn Miller Orchestra played now. Roisin really liked the tune and had taught herself to play it on the piano. However, she resisted the temptation to turn up the volume on the sitting room radio. She didn't think that any of her neighbours in Shandon Park was an informer, but Aunt Nuala insisted on caution, and always played *Radio Freedom* at a low level.

Nuala worked away now at her hobby of painting. She was doing a watercolour of a mountain stream, and they sat listening to the music in companionable silence, then after a moment Roisin's mind began to wander. In two days' time the rescue bid would take place at Liffey Junction, and she prayed that it would be successful and that as many as possible of the prisoners would escape.

Thinking about the prisoners reminded her of her own parents and she fervently hoped that her father was surviving in the work camp in Germany. She turned to her aunt now. 'Can I ask you something?'

'Of course. Though I can't promise I'll be able to answer,' said Nuala with a smile as she lowered her paintbrush.

'It's just, you know the way they say the Allies will invade Western Europe? And that it'll probably be through Ireland?'

'Yes.'

'When would you say that might be?'

Her aunt looked thoughtful. 'That's the big question. Realistically, it would probably have to be in the summer, for an invasion fleet to get the right weather. And it's already June now…'

'So…you don't think it would be this summer?'

'Probably not. I'd say we're talking about late spring, early summer next year. By then the Russians may have gained more ground, and drained German resources further. So I'd say next year.'

'Right,' said Roisin, unable to keep the disappointment from her voice.

'I know it's hard, love, but we have to just hang in for as long as it takes. Your dad is strong, though. When I was a girl I never had to worry, my big brother was the toughest kid around! He's still tough, and he loves you to bits, so I know he'll fight to survive. And your mam is a fighter too. We'll come through this as a family, I just know it.'

Roisin felt a little better, but she still had another concern.

'And what about…what about you and me?'

'How do you mean?'

'You took a big risk, taking me in and getting me false papers and all.'

'You're flesh and blood, darling!'

'I'm still so grateful. But…but supposing it ever unravels. If somehow they find out what you did, and they trace me here?'

'I don't think that will happen. But if it ever starts to look likely, we won't hang about.'

'What would we do?'

'Take to the hills. Literally. The Germans are cock-of-the-walk in the cities and big towns. But they can't be everywhere. And they don't know the countryside the way the locals do. If we had to, we could vanish in Mayo.'

'Yes?'

'We've cousins and friends and neighbours who'd hide us. It would be rough, and we'd only do it as a last resort. But if we have to run for it, that's where we run. Understood?'

'Yes. And thanks. You're…you're just a brilliant aunt.'

'And you're a brilliant niece. Come here to me.'

Nuala hugged her, and Roisin hugged back. She was still worried about the rescue on Monday night, and she wished that she could share her concerns with Nuala. But she couldn't break her word to Mary on staying silent. Instead she said nothing, tried to put her worries aside, and gave herself up to her aunt's warm embrace.

'Nothing to report?' said *Kriminalkommissar* Vogts, his stare challenging as he looked Dennis in the eye. 'I'm not paying you to report nothing.'

Dennis swallowed hard but tried not to show that he felt intimidated. They were seated in a quiet corner of the old city reservoir at Blessington Street. Despite it being a cool, blustery evening, there were other Sunday evening strollers about, so that Vogts kept his voice pitched at a level that didn't draw attention. But his tone was still accusatory, and Dennis had to make a conscious effort not to let his voice waver as he answered the *Gestapo* man.

'I've spent hours on end keeping watch in the Botanics. It's not my fault, *Kommissar,* if there's nothing going on.'

'Or maybe it *is* going on, and you haven't seen it.'

'No, I would have seen it. I've been watching like a hawk.' Dennis thought of all the games of street soccer that he had missed while staking out the Botanic Gardens and he felt annoyed at the German. Part of him suspected that Vogts was deliberately choosing to seem dissatisfied in order to keep him on his toes, and he resented the German's game-playing. Vogts was still frightening, however, and Dennis was careful to be respectful even as he argued his case.

'Just like we change the locations where we meet, probably the people you're hunting are doing the same,' he suggested.

'Maybe,' said Vogts. 'But you're meant to keep your eyes open in general, not just regarding the Botanic Gardens.'

Dennis bit his lip, unsure how to respond. He had heard anti-Nazi chit-chat from patrons in the foyer of the local Bohemian Cinema the previous night, and the staff had simply ignored it. But if he reported this there was the chance that the Germans would close the cinema as a punishment. Dennis loved the westerns and comedies that the Bohemian often showed, and he didn't want to lose out on a cheap source of entertainment.

'Am I failing to make myself clear?' said Vogts.

'No, *Kommissar.* No, you're not,' answered Dennis quickly, fearful now that he had displeased the German. 'Actually…there *was* something, but…but I thought it might be too small to bother you with.'

'No information is too small to bother me with. I told you that at the start.'

'Sorry.'

'So what is this information?'

'The … eh … the usher in the Bohemian Cinema did nothing when people there were making anti-German comments.'

'When was this?'

'Last night.'

'What time?'

'About…about half seven.'

'Very well. That will be followed up.'

Dennis felt a little sorry for the usher, who was friendly and easy-going. *But he should have known better than to get on the wrong side of the Nazis.* And besides, it was more important not to antagonise Vogts than it was to protect a cinema usher.

'Anything else?'

'No, that…that really is it, *Kommissar.*'

Vogts said nothing, then nodded. 'All right.' He discreetly passed Dennis an envelope with his payment. 'Stop the Botanics observation. But keep your eyes and ears open for anything else. I don't want to hear again the words "nothing to report". Understood?'

'Yes, sir, understood.'

'Good. Be on your way then. Rendezvous F, next week.'

Vogts had given Dennis a list of locations, each denoted by a letter from the alphabet so that they could vary where they met.

'F it is,' said Dennis. Then he rose and moved off, glad of the money, but aware that somehow or other, he had to unearth more information for *Kriminalkommissar* Vogts.

PART TWO

JUNE 1943

INSURGENCY

CHAPTER NINE

'I can't sit by, twiddling my thumbs,' said Kevin. 'I've got to do something!'

'Like what?' asked Roisin.

'I'm not sure. But I need to…to take some kind of action.'

They were in the parlour of Roisin's house, its linoleum floor gleaming in the sunlight that beamed in through the window. Kevin disliked Mondays in the classroom, but today he had been totally unfocused, and had received two slaps on the hand with the leather from his teacher, Brother Young. Kevin was normally good at maths, but all day today he had been distracted by the thought of tonight's planned Resistance operation at Liffey Junction.

'It would be different if the raid was happening somewhere down the country,' he continued now, 'but it's only fifteen minutes from here to Liffey Junction. It seems…it seems wrong to do nothing. Do you not feel like that?' he asked Roisin.

'Yes, and I'd love to help. But there's no role for us, Kevin. Mary would have a fit if we just showed up.'

'Not if we got her out of a fix. I've been thinking. Even though she says she can't tell us the details, I'm sure she's playing some sort of part.'

'So what are you saying?'

'Supposing we waited till it got dark, then hid at Liffey Junction?

If everything goes smoothly and Mary doesn't need any help, then grand. But if things get messy and she's in trouble, we'd be there.' Kevin looked at his friend. He sensed from her expression that she was weighing up the benefits of involvement against the risk of being arrested. Suddenly he felt a stab of guilt. If he were caught by the *Gestapo*, his father's contacts might save him. But if Roisin were caught – and especially if her Jewish background came out – the punishment could be lethal.

'Look, I'm not trying to force you into anything,' he said. 'It's just that, well, that day in the Botanics, you said how much you hated the Nazis, and you wished you could fight back.'

'I know.'

'I thought there might be a chance to do that tonight. But I understand if you think it's too risky, really I do.'

Kevin looked at her, one part of him hoping that she would join him, while another part of him thought that maybe he shouldn't have put her on the spot. Either way, though, his own mind was made up. He would slip out after dark and make his way to the site of the raid, with or without Roisin.

She thought a moment more, then looked him in the eye. 'You're right,' she said. 'It's a chance to fight back, and Mary might need our help. I'll do it.'

'Are you sure?'

'Certain. Count me in.'

Kevin felt a surge of affection for his friend. 'Great,' he said. 'Let's think it through, and draw up a plan.'

Mary suppressed a shiver as she crouched in a field by the railway line near Liffey Junction. The June day had been warm, but now the night breeze had a chill to it. In truth, though, it was more than the temperature that made her want to shiver, and she kept her knees together to stop them from trembling. She had insisted to her parents that she wanted to have a role in tonight's operation, but now, as she waited to go into action, she hoped she hadn't made a mistake.

It was one thing to carry messages for the Resistance and to transmit orders from her father. But to be actively involved in an operation against the Germans where shots would be fired – and men probably killed – was different. Maybe Dad's original argument was right, and it *wasn't* a place for a twelve-year-old girl. No! she told herself; she couldn't start thinking like that or she would lose her nerve. Everyone had a role to play in fighting the evil of the Nazis, and she would do what she had to, whatever the cost. She knew that Mam would be really worried until she got safely home, but she had to put that from her mind

She adjusted the curly blonde wig that covered her own black hair. Even though she would be seen only at the start of the operation, that first impression would be critical. *Which meant that a description of her would be given to the Gestapo.* It had been Mary's idea that the character she would assume should speak in a country accent and have curly, blonde hair, when she actually spoke with a Dublin accent and had long, black hair.

'All right, love?' asked her father quietly, giving her shoulder a reassuring squeeze.

'Yes, I'm…I'm fine.'

'Good girl. And Mary?'

'Yes, Dad?'

'I'm really proud of you,' he said, his voice a whisper. 'You're… you're a daughter in a million!'

'Thanks, Dad,' she answered. Her father didn't often speak of his feelings, and Mary was touched by his words. Still nervous, but buoyed now by his praise, she settled back, waiting in the dark shadows for the still-distant train.

Roisin silently crossed the landing, taking care not to wake her aunt. She could hear light snoring from Nuala's bedroom, but she still moved with extreme caution. She began descending the stairs, carefully stepping over the creaky fifth step. Her heart was pounding, both from the tension of trying to sneak soundlessly from the house and from the thought of what lay ahead. But she had agreed to accompany Kevin to Liffey Junction, and there was no backing out now.

She had feigned tiredness and gone to bed a little early, hoping that Aunt Nuala might do likewise. Instead Nuala had stayed up till her normal bedtime of ten-thirty. For Roisin, the time had passed with agonising slowness, until eventually she heard the sound of her aunt's light snores.

It was a quarter past eleven now, and the plan was for Roisin and Kevin to be in position well before the train reached Liffey Junction at five minutes to midnight. She was running late, but to rush now and make a noise that woke Nuala would spell disaster. She knew her aunt would think it was a crazy risk to get involved in a dangerous Resistance operation. And maybe it was foolish. Roisin was tired of being frightened of the Nazis, though, and she wanted to see a blow being struck against them, as well as wanting to support Mary. Besides, some of the prisoners on the train might be Jewish. Roisin thought of her grandmother in London, Hanna Goldberg. The idea of Jewish prisoners like Granny being transported like cattle was horrific, and it was another reason why she had to go to Liffey Junction.

She reached the bottom of the darkened stairs, when suddenly a shape quickly crossed her line of vision. Despite herself, Roisin cried out in shock. Almost immediately she realised it was Gable, the tomcat that Aunt Nuala had adopted. The cat scurried into the parlour, and Roisin was left with her pulses pounding. *How loudly had she cried?* She wasn't sure, and she prayed that she hadn't woken her aunt. She stood unmoving in the hall, straining her ears to hear if Nuala was still asleep. Time seemed to stand still as she waited, dreading the sound of her aunt rising and coming down to investigate. Roisin held her breath, and then slowly exhaled in relief as she heard again the sound of her aunt snoring.

Stepping quietly, she made for the hall door and slowly opened it. She checked that she had her hall door key, then stepped out on to the darkened street. Taking care to do so as gently as possible, she swung the door shut behind her. Then she hurried down the street, eager to meet Kevin and to get to Liffey Junction.

Mary heard the sound of a train in the distance and her heart began to race. 'Dad?' she said, turning to her father. He was crouched beside her in the dark, but she saw the quick shake of his head.

'No, that's a scheduled goods train,' he whispered. 'The one after that is ours.'

'Right.'

Part of Mary felt relieved that the moment of truth hadn't arrived yet. But another part of her wished that it *was* the train carrying the prisoners, so she could get her role in the operation over and done with.

Despite the righteousness of their cause, Mary didn't feel as brave now as she had when she had insisted to Dad that she wanted to be involved. People were likely to die here tonight. *She* could die tonight. But there was no retreating at this stage. She had gone to confession in St Peter's church last Saturday, and while waiting now for the train she had made an Act of Contrition and prayed that their mission would be successful.

The operation itself was the most ambitious Resistance action since the surrender to the Nazis over two years previously. All her father's skills and experience as an army officer had come into play, and Mary was impressed by the scale of what had been put in place. In the darkened fields to the west of Liffey Junction men and trucks were waiting to ferry away the freed prisoners. On the east side of the rail junction, across the canal and railway line, was the land of Broombridge House. These fields too held trucks and armed Resistance fighters, with the residents of Broombridge House and its gate lodge taken prisoner for the duration of the operation. Mary's father had explained that they would be left tied up, so that the *Gestapo* would know that they had been taken captive, and had played no part in the rescue mission.

The plan was that the prisoners from the train would be quickly ferried away, then scattered in smaller groups throughout the country. But first the train had to be stopped, the German guards had to be taken by surprise, and a large group of prisoners freed and led to multiple vehicles. It was an ambitious and risky plan, and Mary knew that if even one part of it went wrong it could end up a blood-soaked disaster.

She saw the headlights of the approaching goods train and she crouched low in the darkness as the locomotive went by. Smoke from the steam engine scented the night air, then the last carriage passed and the train disappeared into the distance.

The quiet of the night returned, and Mary strained her ears, listening anxiously. *The next train was the one.* She breathed out, trying to calm herself. But her heart was pounding and her mouth had gone dry, and she knew that the next few minutes would be the most dangerous ones of her life.

Kevin came to a sudden halt. There were no lights on the canal towpath, and the moon was covered by a bank of cloud, but they were getting close to the Seventh Lock. He and Roisin were dressed in dark clothes so as not to be visible, and she turned to him now.

'What's up?' she whispered.

'We're getting near,' he said, keeping his voice equally low and trying hard not to sound as nervous as he felt. He had deliberately avoided looking at the lighted window of a canal-side cottage that they had passed earlier. Now his night sight was sufficiently keen to make out in the distance the faint outline of the water tower at the Seventh Lock.

'Well, we need to be near, to see what goes on,' said Roisin.

'But not so close that we blunder into whatever's planned.'

'So what do you suggest?'

'Let's get a tiny bit nearer, then hide in the ditch.'

'And after that?'

'After that we see what happens.'

'OK. And Kevin?

'Yes?

'Do you…do you feel scared?'

He hoped his voice hadn't been quivering, and he didn't want to sound like a coward. On the other hand there was no point in lying. 'I do a bit,' he whispered.

'I do too,' admitted Roisin.

Kevin felt better knowing that his friend was frightened also, but before he could say anything more Roisin spoke again.

'But I'm still glad we came,' she said. 'Just in case Mary needs help.'

'Me too,' said Kevin.

'OK, then, will we pick our spot?' said Roisin.

'Yes,' said Kevin, moving carefully forward. 'Let's be ready.'

'All right, Mary, this is it.'

Her father spoke calmly, but Mary was aware of the tension in his voice. They had both heard the sound of an approaching train, and Mary saw that a red stop signal had been activated. She and her father had previously left the field and crossed the footbridge over the canal to get to the railway line, and now Dad quickly hugged her.

'The minute your part is over, make for home.'

'All right.'

'Good luck, darling.'

'Thanks, Dad.'

Mary gave his arm a farewell squeeze, and then stepped away

from her father. She adjusted her blonde wig, lifted the red lantern that she had been given, and started forward along the railway line. The sound of the train was getting louder now, but to Mary's relief she heard it slowing. *So far so good; the driver must have seen the red signal.* But what happened next was the key to taking the Germans by surprise.

Mary knew from Dad that prison trains normally had armed troops on the roofs of the carriages, and if the driver stopped unexpectedly the soldiers would be on guard. Mary's role was to convince the driver that an accident delaying rail traffic had occurred at Liffey Junction.

Her father had said that in military operations small margins could tip the balance. So although the German guards would be outnumbered by the Resistance fighters hidden on both sides of the railway line, the difference between guards mildly frustrated by a delay, and guards on full alert, could be crucial.

Mary had read the famous children's book *The Railway Children*, and it had given her the idea of a child alerting the train driver to an accident. She had persuaded her father that as a twelve-year-old girl she could distract the train driver and the German guards without them feeling a sense of threat. It had sounded good in theory, but now that it was time to put it into practice her stomach was in a knot. She knew that Mam would be praying hard right now and she hoped her prayers would be answered.

She ran forward waving the lantern from side to side. Although slowing, the train was still coming forward. Mary saw sparks flying up into the night sky as the driver applied the brakes, and the screech of metal on metal was added to by the hiss of steam as the train slowed down.

'Stop, please! There's been an accident!' shouted Mary to the driver, making sure to disguise her voice by speaking in a country accent.

She swung the lantern and called again for the train to stop. Her heart was thumping as the locomotive slowly bore down on her like some dark, iron monster, and she knew that the guards on the roof would have their weapons trained upon her. *One nervous sentry who shot first and asked questions later and it would be all over.* She forced the thought from her mind, and concentrated instead on being convincing, as the train finally came to a halt.

'There's been an accident,' said Mary, approaching the cab. 'My daddy's injured!'

By the light of the lantern Mary could see that the cab was occupied by a driver, another railway man carrying a shovel whom she presumed to be the engineer, and a German officer with a drawn pistol in his hand.

'Can you help me please?!' she said, addressing the German and hoping that he spoke English. 'My daddy fell crossing the track. I think his leg is broken and I can't move him!'

For a moment the officer didn't reply, then he breathed out in exasperation.

'Where is this?' he asked.

'About fifty yards down the track, at the Seventh Lock,' answered

Mary. Her voice sounded croaky with nerves, but she hoped that this would seem natural in a girl whose father was badly injured. Despite her fear, she had managed to keep her accent disguised, and she held the lantern so that her face wasn't well illuminated.

The officer jumped down from the cab, and to Mary's relief he no longer aimed the pistol at her. Instead he called out in German to the guards on the roof.

Mary didn't understand what he said but she sensed that he had bought her story. A moment later two soldiers had climbed down from the roof of the nearest carriage. The officer shouted to his men on the roofs of the following carriages and Mary suspected that it was an explanation for why they were stopped. *Please, God*, she thought, *let this work.*

'Now, you lead us to your injured father, yes?' said the German.

'Yes. And thank you for your help,' answered Mary as the two guards from the train fell in behind the officer.

'This way,' she said, turning around and beginning to retrace her steps. She knew that in the next minute either her father's plan would succeed or a lot of people could be dead. Barely daring to breathe, she led the way. She held the lantern ahead of her and led the three Germans back along the track to where her father lay prostrate and groaning in pain.

'I've brought help, Daddy,' she said, her heart pounding in her chest as if it would explode. She stepped aside to allow the German officer to lean down to examine her father. This was the crucial moment, she knew, and suddenly there was a burst of activity. Her father spun round and rose, ramming a pistol against the officer's head, while from the nearby shadows hidden Resistance men rushed the two German soldiers from behind and swiftly overcame them.

'Don't make a sound or I'll blow your brains out!' cried Dad to the officer.

Mary could see the terror in the officer's eyes and he quickly raised his hands in surrender.

Keeping the gun pressed to the German's head, Dad glanced at Mary. 'You've done your part. Go now. Go!'

'OK!'

Mary turned and quickly crossed the footboards of the canal lock. The plan was that she should immediately make for home and safety. But despite the fear that she had been grappling with, something now made her slow her pace. What happened tonight would go down in history. Did she really want to run away and not know the outcome? It would be disobeying her father's orders not to leave. Yet having come this far she couldn't just opt out. Without thinking any further, she followed her instinct, came to a halt, and then hid in the deep shadows, anxious to see what would happen next.

Roisin was dazzled by a sudden burst of light. To her amazement the whole scene at Liffey Junction was illuminated by arc lights.

Crouching in the ditch with Kevin, she could see the halted goods train carrying the prisoners, the railway sidings, and the dark waters of the canal. A voice now rang out through a loudspeaker.

'*Nehmen Sie die Waffen herunter! Nehemen Sie sofort die Waffen herunter!*' 'Throw down your arms! Throw down your arms at once!'

Roisin's stomach tightened in horror as the word *ambush* instinctively ran through her brain. Resistance operations had been betrayed before, and this one could have been compromised too. But hot on the heels of her fear of betrayal came the realisation that the voice wasn't German. Despite the distortion from the loudspeaker, she realised that it was an Irish voice that had called out the order. This time it was the Resistance who had surprised the Nazis, and Roisin's spirits soared as the voice continued.

'*Wir haben Ihre Leute gefangen genommen. Nehmen Sie die Waffen herunter oder sie werden erschossen!*' 'We've taken your men prisoner. Lay down your arms or they'll be shot!

Roisin found herself holding her breath. There were three goods carriages attached to the stationary engine and on the roof on each carriage there were German troops.

'*Sie sind in der Minderheit. Nehmen Sie die Waffen herunter, um eine Schlacht zu vermeiden!*' 'You're completely outnumbered. Lay down your arms to avoid slaughter!

For a split second nobody reacted, then Roisin saw the nearest guard laying down his rifle on the roof of the carriage. But no sooner had he done so than other troops opened fire in the direction of the loudspeaker. Suddenly there was chaos as the resistance volunteers returned fire. There were screams, and Roisin saw one soldier falling from a carriage roof to the ground. Other troops scrambled down off the roofs, and Roisin realised that the Resistance fighters had to be careful with their gunfire so as not to hit the prisoners inside the goods carriages.

There was screaming and shouting and then the sound of glass shattering as one of the searchlights was hit by bullets and was suddenly extinguished.

'Oh my God, look at this!' cried Kevin, and Roisin too was taken aback as she saw how many Resistance fighters were closing in on the carriages. Another searchlight was hit by German fire, creating a dark pocket on the canal bank, and in the chaos Roisin saw a figure ducking low and running in her direction. She had only had a glimpse of him, but a glimpse was all it took for her to recognise the coal-scuttle helmet of a German soldier.

The man was crouched really low but moving at speed, and Roisin calculated that if he wasn't shot in the next couple of seconds he would make it to the darkness of the towpath and escape towards Phibsboro. Roisin reckoned that to free all the prisoners from the carriages and get them to the escape vehicles would take time. Which meant that if the man making for the darkened towpath got away and raised the alarm the Germans could be back before all the prisoners had made their escape.

Please, she thought, *someone stop him!*

In the chaos, however, no shots brought down the escaping

German. With a growing sense of horror Roisin realised it was up to her to act. But she was unarmed and was only half the size of the man. What could she do? She found herself trembling at the thought of grappling with a Nazi soldier, then before she had time to think about it anymore the man drew near. Roisin stayed immobile, then suddenly stuck out her leg as the German ran past. The man tripped, falling heavily to the ground. Acting purely on instinct now, Roisin jumped to her feet. The German was groggily starting to rise when she reached him, and Roisin grabbed him by the lapels and pushed him forward, her momentum bringing them both to the canal bank.

The man cried out what Roisin suspected was a swear word in German, but she paid no heed. Pushing with all her strength, she heaved him over the edge and was rewarded with a loud splash as the soldier fell into the canal.

'Over here!' cried Roisin. 'There's a German soldier in the canal! Over here!'

More Resistance fighters were emerging from the field on the canal side of the railway and several of them ran to the canal bank. They dragged the soldier from the water and took him prisoner, and one of the Resistance men looked at Roisin quizzically. 'What are you doing here?' he asked.

'That's…that's a long story. Just be glad I stopped him escaping,' she answered. Then she turned back to Kevin, and they stepped away into the darkness.

Mary had never felt so exhilarated. For once the Irish were winning and the Nazis were losing. The shooting had stopped now and freed prisoners were spilling from the goods carriages. In the light from the remaining arc lamps she could see that several German soldiers were lying dead and wounded beside the railway track, while the rest of their comrades had surrendered.

Mary stepped out of her hiding place, eager to take in the details of what looked like a dramatic victory. Despite the apparent chaos of scores of prisoners jumping down onto the tracks, she knew that the operation had been planned with painstaking attention to detail. Already freed prisoners were being quickly ushered to the waiting trucks on both sides of the canal, while the captive German guards had been disarmed and were being handcuffed to the doors of the railway carriages.

'Mary, I thought you'd gone home!'

She spun around to see her father had suddenly materialised from behind her. She saw the look of concern on his face and felt bad at adding to his concerns.

'Sorry. But…I just had to see what was happening.' She hoped her father wouldn't be too angry with her. 'I'm…I'm sorry, Dad.'

But instead of being angry he looked worried. 'You've got to get to safety! We don't know how soon the Germans will get here.'

'All right.'

'Go now, love. Run all the way home!' He quickly squeezed her arm in farewell, then pointed towards the towpath leading back to

Phibsboro. 'Go!'

Mary wanted to hug him and to tell him to take care, but she knew that she had already distracted him. Instead she squeezed his arm and whispered 'I love you, Dad.' Then she ran to the lock and crossed the footboards.

Freed prisoners were being lead across the lock by Resistance fighters, and Mary felt a sense of pride that her father's rescue bid was succeeding. Turning right, she stepped out of the light from the arc lamps, her eyes struggling to adjust to the darkness.

'Mary!' called a voice. 'Over here!'

To her amazement, she recognised Kevin's voice. She stopped. 'Kevin?'

'And me,' said Roisin.

Her friends appeared out of the darkness.

'What…what are you doing here?' said Mary.

'We knew you'd be here and we…we just wanted to make sure you'd be OK,' said Kevin.

Mary felt a surge of affection. 'You're…you're brilliant friends. I can't believe you did that. But being here is risky.'

'The rescue is working, though, isn't it?' said Roisin.

'Yes. But the shooting will have been heard, so more Germans will arrive. It's a race against time.'

'And your part is finished?' said Kevin.

'Yes.'

'Then we should get out of here.'

'That's what I was about to do.'

'Let's not dawdle then,' said Roisin. 'Let's run for home.'

'OK!'

Mary took a last glance at the floodlit scene behind her, then she turned away and sprinted off into the darkness.

CHAPTER TEN

'Who the Hell do they think they are, making everyone's life a misery?!' demanded Dennis's father across the breakfast table.

Ma and Dennis's two sisters knew better than to argue when Da was annoyed, and everyone nodded in agreement. In truth Dennis agreed with his father, who was furious at the Resistance for the previous night's raid at Liffey Junction.

Up to now Nazi reprisals hadn't affected the family too much – although The Bohemian Cinema had been closed for two weeks as a punishment for allowing the anti-Nazi talk that Dennis had secretly reported. Last night, though, was different, and thirty Irishmen were to be shot in a ten-to-one reprisal for the three German soldiers who had died at Liffey Junction. It was a brutal demonstration that Ireland was a defeated, occupied country. Dennis's sisters were shaken, and had pointed out that no-one was safe, and that *their* family could have been among those chosen for execution.

'Making their gestures while other people pay the price!' said Da, continuing his rant about the Resistance. 'Why can't they drop the false heroics and face reality?'

Dennis nodded again, although he felt that anyone who went up against the Nazis, however foolishly, wasn't wanting in courage.

Better not say that to Da, though, he thought.

'It's the families of the hostages I feel sorry for,' said Ma. 'Being shot for something you didn't do, that's awful.'

'The Resistance know the Nazis will kill people in reprisals – and yet they go ahead. I blame them as much as the Germans.' Da looked around the table, as though challenging anyone to disagree with him.

Time to get out, thought Dennis, *you never knew how things would turn out when Da was in this sort of mood.* 'I'd better head off to school,' he said, rising from the table. 'Might take longer than usual this morning.'

After last night's train incident the streets of Phibsboro and Cabra had been swamped with *Gestapo* officers and German troops. Cordons had been set up, and houses were being violently searched as the Nazis reacted furiously to the freeing of almost two hundred prisoners at Liffey Junction.

Dennis's sisters and his father had complained about having to allow more time than usual to get to work in the city centre. But Dennis thought there was a certain excitement to what had happened, and he was in good spirits as he bid his family goodbye. He stepped out the door into hazy sunshine and looked down Leinster Street.

In the distance he could see a cordon at the junction of Phibsboro Road and Leinster Street. Despite what he had said at home he didn't actually care if he got held up and was late for classes. It was the final week of term in the vocational school, and already the teachers had relaxed as the year wound down and the summer holidays drew nearer.

He thought again about last night's train raid. Rumours had spread like wildfire that a girl had been involved, and now every girl between the ages of eight and fourteen who lived in Phibsboro or Cabra was to be questioned. Dennis hoped that it would put the fear of God into Roisin Tierney and Mary Flanagan. Ever since the arm-twisting incident with Kevin Burke, the girls had been cool with him. Well, let's see how long they'd maintain their stuck-up act when the *Gestapo* cross-examined them. The idea made him smile, and he approached the cordon confidently.

Dennis saw that German troops in a half-track had blocked the road, but that the pedestrian check-point was being manned by uniformed Irish policemen, supervised by a plainclothes *Gestapo* officer.

'Name and address?' asked one of the policemen.

'Dennis O'Sullivan, 57 Leinster Street North.'

'And your business?'

Dennis thought this was a silly question, considering the schoolbag on his back. He was tempted to give a smart answer, but stopped himself. The authorities had been made to look foolish by the raid last night and would be spoiling for a fight. 'Just going to the tech,' he replied pleasantly.

'Right, on your way then,' said the policeman self-importantly.

Dennis nodded in reply, idly wondering if the man was trying to impress the nearby *Gestapo* officer or if he was just a mini-

Napoleon who liked to exert authority. Before he could decide, a volley of shots rang out. Dennis started, though not as much as the policeman who looked around wildly.

'*Einsatzgruppen*,' said the nearest Gestapo officer, making no effort to hide his disapproval of the policeman's nervous reaction.

Dennis knew that *Einsatzgruppen* were the Nazis mobile killing units, and he realised that the shots were from the nearby Mount-joy Jail. *They haven't lost any time*, thought Dennis grimly, if these were the first executions in reprisal for the soldiers killed at Liffey Junction.

Dennis walked on, his mind racing. Clearly there was going to be a big backlash against last night's action. As a senior *Gestapo* man, Vogts would be furious – which made him dangerous. But rather than suffering his ire, maybe Dennis could score points with him. Supposing he were to take the initiative? Instead of waiting for their next scheduled meeting, he could go to Fitzgibbon Street Station, as he had the first time, and ask to speak to *Kriminalkommissar* Vogts. He could offer his support in trying to unearth the culprits from last night. Vogts was a powerful man, and it would do no harm to be on his good side. Even if nothing came of the offer, it would still be a smart gesture to make.

Yes, thought Dennis, let other people worry about the backlash from last night's raid – he would turn it to his advantage. Pleased with his decision, he headed for school with a spring in his step.

Kevin knew that eavesdropping was rude, but he couldn't help himself. He had just finished brushing his teeth before going to school, and on coming out of the bathroom he stopped on the landing. He heard his father speaking on the telephone in the spare bedroom that he used as an office. Dad's manner was normally affable but this morning he sounded agitated.

'I have to *live here*, Major Weber!' he said. 'As a councillor, people expect me to protect them, and feelings are running high.'

Kevin listened, fascinated.

'I *know* reprisals are policy, Major. I don't like it, but I understand it. But it's one thing killing Resistance prisoners, it's another thing shooting civilians.'

There was a pause, and Kevin wished he knew what Major Weber was saying. He had disliked him when they had met in the Rainbow Restaurant, but Dad had claimed he was one of the more reasonable Nazis.

'It's easy for you to say it's out of your hands, Major!' continued Kevin's father. 'But one of the civilians rounded up is from Connaught Street. That makes him practically a neighbour of mine.'

Kevin knew nothing of this, and was shocked that a local man had already been targeted for execution.

'I see…' said Dad. 'Well, I'm very disappointed to hear that, Major, very disappointed. Good morning to you.'

Kevin heard his father hanging up, then a moment later he stepped out onto the landing, his expression uncharacteristically hard. 'Kevin…' he said. 'Were you…were you listening?'

'I'm sorry, Dad, I couldn't help hearing. Are they going to shoot someone from Connaught Street?'

His father nodded wearily. 'I'm afraid so.'

'Who is it?'

'A man called Sean Murray. I don't know him personally. Not that it would change their minds if I did.'

'And he's nothing to do with the Resistance?'

'No, he was chosen at random.'

'Why would they do that?'

'To punish the population at large. Cabra and Phibsboro are the two nearest areas to Liffey Junction, so they've taken civilians as part of the reprisals.'

'That's just…that's so wrong.'

'I know, Kevin, but they think shooting Resistance prisoners doesn't deter other Resistance people. They've *already* decided to risk their lives. Whereas killing civilians intimidates the population as a whole.'

'Even though they did nothing?'

His father nodded. 'It's to make sure other people aren't tempted to do anything in future.'

Kevin felt sickened by the cold-bloodedness of the Nazis. But he also felt a touch of personal guilt. If he hadn't tipped off the Resistance about the prisoner train, the operation wouldn't have taken place, and Sean Murray and others wouldn't be facing execution. In his heart of hearts, Kevin had known that reprisals were likely in the aftermath of the raid. Yet if he had done nothing the

Irish Jews and the other prisoners on the train – almost two hundred people – would have ended up dead in Germany.

'It's an awful situation, son, and I'm sorry you've been exposed to it.'

If you only knew, thought Kevin. Yet despite his disgust at the Nazis' tactics, and the high price being paid, he still felt on balance that he had done the right thing.

'Are you all right?' asked Dad gently.

'Yes, I'm…I'm OK.'

'Best head off to school then. Try and keep things as normal as possible.'

Kevin thought that things could never be normal again until the Nazis had been defeated, but there was no point saying that to his father. 'Right, I'll get my bag,' he answered, then he started down the stairs, his mind a whirl as he tried to come to terms with all that was happening.

'Don't be apologetic,' said Aunt Nuala, 'and don't act like you're worried. On the other hand don't be cocky to the point of drawing attention.'

'OK,' said Roisin.

'Just answer their questions like you've nothing to be concerned about.'

'All right.'

Roisin and her aunt were at the kitchen table, the hazy morning sunshine softly lighting the room. Aunt Nuala was coaching her in preparation for her questioning by the Germans, and Roisin listened to her advice, knowing that any kind of slip-up could be fatal.

'You were asleep in bed all night,' continued Nuala, 'and you know nothing about what happened.'

Roisin nodded, feeling guilty about deceiving her aunt, yet unable to betray the secret of Mary and Commandant Flanagan's Resistance involvement.

'You don't know any girl who fits the description that's leaked out,' said Nuala, 'and you've heard no rumours of who it might be. Give them nothing whatsoever.'

'I won't,' said Roisin.

'And don't worry, love, you'll just be one of hundreds of girls that they question.'

'I know. I'd better go, I told Mary I'd call for her.'

Roisin rose, and her aunt came around the table and gave her a hug.

'Good luck, pet. Not that you need it. I know you'll be fine.'

'Thanks,' said Roisin, and then she nodded in farewell and headed for the door.

She stepped out into the June morning and walked the few yards down the road to Mary's house. At the far end of the road she could see German soldiers carrying out house-to-house searches, but she tried not to let their presence unsettle her. She suspected that the searches were prompted more by way of punishment than from a belief that the escaped prisoners would be hidden in the Shandon Park area. There was no doubt, however, that the Nazis were furious about the raid. The fact that they were preparing to question hundreds of girls showed how determined they were. There was also the awful response of reprisals, and Roisin had been sickened earlier when she heard the volley of shots from Mountjoy Jail.

But all that had to be put aside for the moment – she needed to concentrate on her own interrogation.

Reaching Mary's house, she knocked on the door. It was only about ten hours since she and Mary had breathlessly run back here in the dark after the raid, yet already it seemed like an incident from another time and place. Both she and Mary had quietly let themselves in and been in bed within minutes. Roisin had thanked her stars that Aunt Nuala was a heavy sleeper, but she herself had lain awake for a long time, her mind buzzing after the exhilaration of the train rescue. Eventually she had drifted into a deep sleep, only to be woken early by the arrival of large numbers of German troops. House searches had begun and the *Gestapo* had drawn up lists of girls aged between eight and fourteen. Both she and Mary had been scheduled for a 10.30 a.m. interrogation in St Peter's School, and now her friend opened the door.

'Ready?' said Roisin.

'As I'll ever be,' answered Mary grimly.

Roisin reached out and squeezed her arm reassuringly. 'It'll be all right, Mary. You said yourself they didn't get a good look at your face in the dark. And they'll be watching for a blonde girl with a country accent. Neither of us is blonde, and we can lay on the Dublin accents.'

'I know. But those *Gestapo* men, they make my skin crawl.'

'They make everyone's skin crawl,' said Roisin, as they started down the road. 'But they're like all bullies. The way to deal with them is to act like you're not afraid.'

'You're right,' said Mary. 'OK, let's look them in the eye, and brazen it out.'

'Yes,' said Roisin, pleased that she had lifted her friend's spirits. They turned into Shandon Road, reliving last night's adventures and speculating on where the escapers might be by now. So far there was no word of any of them being recaptured, and Roisin congratulated her friend on how brilliantly Commandant Flanagan had organised the operation.

Crossing Connaught Street, they entered St Peter's Road, and Roisin felt her pulse beginning to race as they approached St Peter's School. Police vehicles were parked outside the building and other girls, their expressions nervous, entered the school with Roisin and Mary.

They came into a hallway that was humming with activity as unformed policemen took the details of each arrival and checked them against typed lists.

'Name?' asked a heavyset policeman with a lilting Cork accent.

'Mary Flanagan, 4 Shandon Park.'

'And you, love?'

Roisin realised that the policeman was trying to be sympathetic, and she made her tone friendly. 'Roisin Tierney, 10 Shandon Park.'

'Just wait a minute, girls, and you'll be told where to go.'

'OK', said Mary. The policeman moved on to another group of girls, and Roisin turned away. Her gaze fell on a well-built man standing at the far end of the room. 'Oh my God!' she said quietly, her stomach suddenly tightening in fear

'What is it?' asked Mary.

'The…the *Gestapo* man who nearly caught me in Cork,' whispered Roisin. 'He's here!'

'What?'

'That's him,' said Roisin. 'That's him at the end of the room!' No sooner had Roisin said it than the man looked in their direction. Then he stepped forward and walked directly towards them.

Mary breathed deeply, trying hard to appear calm. The *Gestapo* man was definitely making for them, and Mary prayed that he hadn't recognised Roisin. *After all, her friend had escaped from Cork over two years ago.* Roisin had said that she and the *Gestapo* man had never actually come face to face back then, and Mary told herself that the German must have seen pictures of thousands of wanted people since then.

Mary glanced at Roisin and was pleased to see that her expression gave nothing away. She knew that her friend must be terrified, but she wasn't panicking, and Mary resolved that she wouldn't either.

'Your names?' said the German, coming to a halt before the two girls.

He had a strong physical presence, with close-cropped hair and eyes that had a penetrating gaze. Mary sensed that this man would be a formidable foe, and that she couldn't afford to drop her guard for even an instant.

'Mary Flanagan,' she answered, remembering to play up her Dublin accent.

'Roisin Tierney.'

Mary swallowed hard. If the man remembered Roisin as an escaped Jew it would be fatal for her. *To say nothing of how it would be for Mary as her companion.*

The German said nothing for a moment then he pointed at Roisin. 'Go to room B2 and wait your turn to be questioned.' Roisin caught Mary's eye and nodded in farewell, and Mary felt a surge of relief that the man didn't seem to have recognised her friend. Then he turned and pointed at Mary herself. 'And you, you come with me.'

She felt her heart thumping but tried to show no fear. 'All right so.'

The *Gestapo* man looked at her challengingly 'I wasn't giving you a choice.'

Before Mary could think of how to respond the German called

to an Irish policeman who was passing with a clipboard of names. 'You there!'

'Yes, *Kommissar* Vogts?'

'I want somewhere quiet for an interview.'

'Eh…perhaps the principal's office?'

'Where is that?'

'Down the corridor, sir, last door on the right.'

While the two men spoke, Mary's mind was racing. So the German's name was Vogts, and he was a *Kriminalkommissar*, which she knew was a fairly senior rank in the *Gestapo*. But why did he want to interview her privately?

'Follow me,' he ordered, and Mary fell into step behind him. He moved with the ease of an athlete as he strode down the school corridor, away from the noise of the reception hall. Without knocking, he entered the principal's office, which was vacant. The room had battered filing cabinets, and the walls had mounted photographs of football teams, as well as the obligatory portrait of Adolph Hitler.

Vogts sat behind the principal's desk and pointed. 'Stand before me,' he instructed.

Mary saw that there was a spare chair for visitors, and she realised that Vogts was deliberately trying to make her feel unsettled. *Well, let him play his games – if he had any hard evidence she would already be arrested.* She took her place without argument, but resolved to stick rigidly to her story.

'Do you know why you're here?' asked Vogts.

'Because all girls my age are being questioned.'

'And why is that?'

'I don't know, sir.'

'You don't know? You've heard nothing about what's happened?'

'I heard there was shooting last night. That something happened at Liffey Junction.'

'Which is close to where you live.'

'It's…it's about a twenty-minute walk away.'

'Oh, you've timed it, have you?'

'No, sir.'

'Then how do you know how long it takes to get there?'

'I've often gone for walks along the canal with my friends. I'm guessing it would be about twenty minutes away.'

Vogts sat forward and looked her directly in the eye. 'Were you there last night?'

Mary forced herself to hold his gaze. 'No, I wasn't.'

Vogts continued to stare at her, and Mary knew that he was looking for any sign of guilt or uncertainty.

'Don't lie to me,' said the German.

'Why would I lie?' answered Mary, deciding to push back a little.

'Because you're the daughter of Patrick Flanagan. A man who died fighting against our forces. Maybe you bear a grudge. Maybe you think resisting would honour his memory. You tell me.'

So that was why she had been earmarked like this, thought Mary.

She paused a moment, rehearsing in her head the explanation on which she and Mam had agreed. 'There's nothing to tell. Our family were heartbroken when he died. We've learnt our lesson. We know now that there's no point in resisting.'

Once again Vogts stared hard at her. 'Really?' he said, as though unconvinced.

'Yes, sir. Our family have paid a big price. We don't want any more trouble.'

'And yet. There's a girl your age who *does* want trouble. Who played a role in last night's operation.'

'I don't know anything about that, sir.'

'So you keep saying. What time did you hear the gunfire?' he asked, suddenly changing tack.

'I didn't hear the gunfire.'

'You said earlier you heard shooting last night.'

'No, sir. I said I heard that there *was* shooting. I didn't hear it though, I slept through the night.'

'Come closer,' ordered Vogts. 'Lower your head and spread out your hair on the desk.'

Mary obeyed, and she felt revulsion when she felt Vogts' hand on her hair. But another part of her felt triumphant. *They were looking for a blonde girl. And Vogts must be checking that her raven black hair hadn't been dyed — which it clearly hadn't.*

'All right, you may lift your head,' said the German.

Mary did so, and looked him in the eye.

'If you know anything about this, anything at all, and you don't tell me now, your family will pay a very high price,' he said.

'I don't know anything, sir.'

'That's all you have to say for yourself?'

Time to mislead him if possible, thought Mary. 'There is one thing, sir.'

'What?'

'This girl last night at Liffey Junction. It doesn't follow that she's from around here. Surely she could have come from anywhere in Ireland?'

Mary could see at once that Vogts had been hoping for something more than this.

'When I need your advice on police work I'll ask for it!' he snapped.

'Yes, sir,' said Mary with mock humility.

Vogts said nothing for a long moment, before seeming to reach a decision. He indicated the door with a flick of his wrist. 'You may go.'

'Thank you, sir,' said Mary. She stepped out of the office, closed the door after her and breathed a sigh of relief. Then she allowed herself a tiny smile of satisfaction and walked off down the corridor.

CHAPTER ELEVEN

ennis thought the smell of frying rashers was the most mouth-watering smell in the world. He loved Saturday tea, when his mother always did a fry with rashers, sausages and black pudding. Since the introduction of rationing for clothes and food many people looked shabby and undernourished, but if the O'Sullivans' ration coupons didn't stretch to a good fry, then the ingredients were bought on the black market. Da insisted that as a hard-working family they were entitled to some rewards, and their tradition of a Saturday fry-up was one of them.

Dennis was seated at the table now with his parents and his sisters, Frances and Anne.

'Isn't it really sad about Mr Murray from Connaught Street?' said Annie. 'I heard his family got his remains back today.'

'I'd say his funeral mass will be crowded,' said Ma.

'Maybe so,' said Da. 'But we won't be at it.'

Dennis was surprised, and he saw the confusion in his mother's face too.

'But we always get eleven Mass in St Peter's,' she said.

'We won't this Sunday,' said his father firmly. 'We'll get mass in Berkley Road.'

'Why are we switching to Berkley Road, Da?' asked Frances.

Dennis watched as his father took a mouthful of tea before

responding.

'Isn't it obvious? Sean Murray was shot by the Nazis as a reprisal. So there'll be people *packing* that funeral, as a form of protest. We don't want to be seen as part of that.'

'But if we're just going to Mass in the normal way, Da—' began Annie.

'Are you thick or what?!' he said, interrupting her. 'The Germans are in charge. And they're on the warpath after what's happened. We don't show them *any* reason to think we're against them. Everyone who's smart will give that funeral a wide berth.'

Dennis thought Da was taking caution to extremes, but he knew better than to challenge him. Admittedly the last few days had been tension-filled, with the escaped prisoners still at large with the exception of two escapees who had been shot dead by German troops in the Wicklow Mountains. The success of the Resistance operation had been humiliating for the Nazis, but Dennis felt that he had scored points with *Kriminalkommissar* Vogts by offering his services in any way Vogts saw fit.

Vogts had told him to keep his eyes and ears open for the slightest clue regarding the escape operation and its aftermath, and Dennis had readily agreed.

Now, though, Dennis's freedom of movement was being curtailed by Da's decision to avoid the Mass in St Peter's. Dennis had thought the mass would be an excellent opportunity to listen in on the people present – people who might speak a little too freely at the funeral mass.

None of his family knew of Dennis's secret role, so he could hardly explain why he wanted to attend St Peter's. And any kind of direct challenge to his father's authority would be disastrous. *Was there some way that he could persuade him?* he wondered.

'It's so wrong what the Germans did,' said Frances. 'I heard Mr Murray was a lovely man who never had a bad word for anyone,'

'Yes, I heard that too,' said Ma. 'People are really upset.'

'The Germans are turning the whole community against themselves,' said Anne.

Da shrugged. 'The Nazis have the power. They don't care what people think.'

Dennis thought he saw an opening, but he would have to tread carefully. 'Maybe...maybe *we* should care though, Da.' he said.

'How do you mean?'

'Well, I think you're dead right about the family not being seen to be anti-Nazi. But at the same time, maybe it's smart not to be *too* at odds with everyone around us. So I have a suggestion.'

'Have you now?' said Da.

'Supposing...supposing you all go to mass in Berkley Road. But I go to St Peter's. That way if the Germans are recording which families turned out in support we won't be on any list. But if I make sure the neighbours see me, they'll assume the rest of the O'Sullivans were in the church, even though you won't be.'

Dennis looked at his father, struggling to read his expression.

'I've tried to learn from you, Da,' he said, laying on the flattery. 'And you always say we should play things smart. Well this way we get the best of both worlds, don't we?'

Dennis paused, sensing that to push it any further would be a mistake.

His father chewed the last piece of his sausage without saying anything, and then turned back to Dennis. 'All right,' he answered finally. 'I wouldn't be losing too much sleep over what the neighbours think. But having the best of both worlds, that makes sense.'

'So you'll go to Berkley Road and I'll go to St Peter's?'

'Yes.'

'Great,' said Dennis, then he went back happily to finish his fry.

Kevin felt uncomfortable as the congregation milled around in the sunshine outside St Peter's church. Although he wasn't particularly religious, he normally liked Sunday morning Mass. He loved the singing of the choir, the soaring, swirling notes from the organ, and the sense of occasion, with everyone in the congregation making an effort and dressing in their best clothes.

Today had been different. He had never seen the church so full before, and there had been an unmistakable air of protest in the demeanour of the packed congregation at Sean Murray's funeral mass. Mrs Murray, dressed all in black, had looked gaunt but dignified throughout the service, and had been flanked by her two grown-up daughters.

Normally a funeral mass wouldn't have taken place on a Sunday.

The Catholic Church was wary in its dealing with the occupying Nazis, but Kevin sensed that the clergy at St Peter's were making a point by having the funeral mass for the executed local man as the centre point of Sunday services.

Kevin looked about, seeking any of his friends. His parents were talking to Mr Shanahan, the family dentist, but Kevin was aware of a general coolness towards his father. People who might normally have approached and chatted were keeping their distance. Up to now most of the neighbours seemed to have accepted that Councillor Burke had to deal with the Nazis.

Today, though, feelings were running high after the reprisal executions. Nobody had actually said anything negative to the Burkes, but Kevin sensed that his father was a focal point – however unfairly – for the anger people felt at the executions, and a couple of Mam's violin students had cancelled lessons.

Inside the church Kevin had spotted Roisin, her Aunt Nuala, and Dennis O'Sullivan. Dennis had brusquely acknowledged him with a nod, but Kevin and Roisin had exchanged a look. Both of them knew that Sean Murray wouldn't have been executed if Kevin hadn't passed on the information about the prisoner train to Mary. However much he told himself that they had saved many lives, and that the Nazis were the guilty ones for executing civilians, Kevin still felt bad about the hostages that had been shot.

Mr Shanahan made his apologies now and left Kevin's parents, and for a moment the Burkes stood alone in the crowd outside the door of the church. Suddenly Kevin saw Mary approaching.

"Morning, Kevin, Mr and Mrs Burke.'

Kevin's parents returned her greeting, and Kevin felt a surge of affection for his friend. The Flanagans were a family that were clearly not pro-German, and Mary was making a public statement by obviously socialising with the Burkes at a moment when others were shunning them. Kevin thought there were many reasons to loathe the Nazis, but high on his list was the effect they had had on Irish people's behaviour. The population had been split into camps, with a small minority fighting on with the Resistance, and another minority actively collaborating with the occupying power. Most people muddled through, having to make awkward compromises in order to survive, and Kevin hated the divisive way people from different groups were suspicious of their fellow citizens.

Mary continued chatting with his parents for a moment, and then turned to him. 'All right, Kevin?'

Was he all right? Yes, he decided. No matter how sad he was for the victims of the Nazi reprisals, he had done the right thing in providing the information that led to the prisoners being rescued.

'Yes,' he answered, 'Thanks, Mary,' he said, looking her meaningfully in the eye, 'everything's OK.'

CHAPTER TWELVE

oisin didn't often win arguments with her aunt, and she was pleased with herself for bringing Nuala around to her way of thinking. Tonight was the first youth club night since the funeral Mass, and the June evening was warm and bright as she walked towards the club. She was accompanied by Kevin and Mary, and all three were wearing black armbands as a sign of mourning.

Roisin was far from sure that Mr Cox would allow the gesture, and she thought back to earlier when she had entered the kitchen and Nuala had seen the armband.

'Take that off, Roisin,' she had said.

'Other people are wearing them.'

'Family members in mourning. Or people attending funerals. Wearing it to the youth club is completely different.'

'Loads of the members are going to wear them tonight.'

'Out situation's different,' said Nuala. 'So far, we've gotten away with changing your identity. But we can't attract attention.'

'But if most members are wearing the armbands, and I *don't*, that could look a bit odd. *That* could attract attention.'

Roisin could see that her aunt hadn't thought of it that way, and she pushed ahead while she thought she had an advantage. 'Look, if Mr Cox says we can't wear them at the club I'll take it off. Immediately. But if the others are all wearing them, I'll hardly draw special attention by wearing one too.'

Aunt Nuala appeared thoughtful, and Roisin looked to her appealingly. 'Please. It's what Mr de Valera would want.'

Roisin knew that her aunt was a big admirer of the politician, Éamon de Valera. He had been the head of government at the time of the German invasion, and had escaped from Ireland at the last minute when Dublin fell to the Nazis. Now he was the leader of the Irish government-in-exile in Washington, and tonight Roisin and Nuala had sat by the radio with the volume turned low as de Valera had broadcast on *Radio Freedom*. De Valera had claimed that the Allies were fighting back successfully, with the Americans inflicting heavy losses on the Japanese Navy in the Pacific, the Russians pushing back the Nazis on the Eastern Front, and the British and Americans defeating the German U-boats in the Battle of the Atlantic. He exhorted the Irish people not to lose hope, and to resist Nazi rule until the day that Ireland could be liberated.

'Please, Aunt Nuala. They've split up our family, they've taken our country, they're shooting hostages. I know the armband is only a small thing, but I have to do *something* in reply.'

Although she still had misgivings, Nuala had relented, and now Roisin crossed the busy Phibsboro Road with her friends. As they made for the hall where the youth club held its Friday night meetings, Roisin's mood was nervous yet buoyant.

In the past few days two of the escaped prisoners had been

recaptured in Wexford, and one had been shot dead in the Knock-mealdown Mountains. Almost two hundred men still remained at large, however, and the Irish population had been given a lift, despite the widespread anger at the executions carried out in reprisal.

Arriving at the club, Roisin saw lots of other members hanging about outside the locked door.

'Not like Mr C to be late opening,' said Mary.

'We're actually three minutes early,' said Kevin, consulting the wristwatch that Roisin knew he had been given by his parents for his last birthday.

She looked at the waiting members, more interested in whether or not they were wearing armbands than in Mr Cox's punctuality. Dennis O'Sullivan and his friends Terry Lawless and Peadar Feeney were engaging in horseplay and none of them wore armbands. Neither did several other members, but a quick calculation told Roisin that about two thirds of members did.

She was pleased by the response, but before she had time to think about it any further Kevin spoke up.

'Here's Mr Cox!'

The shopkeeper arrived, jingling a bunch of keys in his hands. 'Sorry for keeping you, boys and girls, slight problem at the shop.'

'Everything OK, now, Mr C?' asked Mary

'Yes, Mary,' he answered. Then he paused, the keys in his hand.

Roisin knew that he had taken in the fact that so many of the club members were wearing black armbands. In theory, they could claim to be still wearing them as a sign of mourning. In reality though, there was a definite undercurrent of protest against the executions.

Mr Cox looked uncertain, and Roisin felt sympathy for him. As a shopkeeper trying to run a business in a German-occupied city he could ill afford to alienate the Nazis. But as a native of Phibsboro he couldn't but have felt disgust at the cold-blooded execution of his neighbour, Sean Murray.

He hesitated for a moment, and Roisin exchanged glances with Kevin and Mary. They had taken a risk in donning the armbands, and it would be humiliating now to be told to take them off, especially in front of someone like Dennis O'Sullivan.

Mr Cox paused, and Roisin sensed that he wasn't going to run the risk of crossing the Germans. He opened his mouth to speak, but seemed to struggle to find the right words. Roisin found herself holding her breath, then Mr Cox appeared to make up his mind.

'OK, in we go,' he said, turning the key in the lock and opening the door.

Roisin felt a surge of admiration for him and wanted to cheer – but she knew she couldn't do that. Instead she winked at Kevin and Mary, then walked into the club.

The rippling waters of the River Tolka caught the evening sun as Dennis made his way to his Sunday evening rendezvous with *Kriminalkommissar* Vogts. Dennis entered Griffith Park from Botanic Avenue, rehearsing in his head what he would report this evening. His first instinct had been to reveal the black armband wearing that Mr Cox had allowed on Friday night. It was a minor gesture of defiance, admittedly, but Vogts had said that no sign of resistance to German rule was too small to report. It also had the attraction of possibly getting Kevin Burke. Roisin Tierney, and Mary Flanagan into trouble.

Even before their coolness to him after the arm-twisting incident, he had never liked the trio of friends. Although Dennis's father was a foreman printer in the *Irish Press*, he was still a tradesman, whereas Mrs Tierney and Mr Burke had white collar jobs, and Captain Flanagan had been an officer in the army. What with their better jobs, and the fact that their houses in Shandon Park were slightly more upmarket than his one in Leinster Street, Dennis felt that Roisin, Kevin, and Mary looked down on him. *But they wouldn't be so full of themselves if they were taken into custody by the Gestapo.*

On balance, though, Dennis had reluctantly decided not to report Mr Cox. In reality, Mr Cox was more likely to be punished than the youthful members, and Dennis didn't want that. He had been looking forward to the club's annual camp – to be held this year in County Galway – and if Mr Cox was arrested or barred from running the club, the trip might be cancelled.

Dennis moved through the greenery of the park, then saw Vogts sitting on one of the benches that overlooked the Tolka. There weren't too many people in this part of the park, but Vogts paid no attention when Dennis sat on the far end of the bench. The German appeared to continue reading the newspaper, and spoke in a low voice. 'Well?'

'I went to eleven o'clock mass this morning in St Peter's,' said Dennis. 'The priest gave a sermon on loving your fellow man. And he came right out and said that recent Nazi behaviour in Dublin was anti-Christian.'

'Did he now?' said Vogts. 'Was this the parish priest?'

'No, the PP is always careful what he says. This was Father Graham.'

'Tell me more about him.'

'He's fairly young, but he's kind of cocky.'

'These Catholic priests,' said Vogts irritably, 'they think they're untouchable. Well, *Father Graham* will soon learn otherwise!'

Vogts hadn't lowered the newspaper, but Dennis could imagine the disdain on his face. It was clear that the German had a problem with Catholicism, and Dennis made a mental note of Vogts' attitude. 'What else?'

'Eh, I heard rumours that black market food is being sold on Friday nights, when people get their pay packets.'

'Sold where?'

'In the grounds of The Albert College. It could be just a rumour, of course, but I thought you'd want to know.'

'You did well to tell me,' said Vogts, his tone warmer. 'We'll check it out.'

'Right.'

'Anything else?'

'No, I think that's about it,' said Dennis.

'Really? That's quite disappointing.'

Dennis was taken aback by Vogts' switch from approval to disapproval. *Don't be taken aback,* he told himself. *The Gestapo specialise in keeping people off balance.*

'You live near Liffey Junction. I thought by now you'd have heard some whispers about the night of the train attack,' the German said.

'People are frightened. No one is talking about it.'

'That's hard to believe,' said Vogts dismissively. 'Children blabber all the time. *Somebody* must know *something* about the girl who stopped the train.'

'But, *Kommisar*, she could be from anywhere. Belfast, Cork, Galway, Limerick. It's a needle in a haystack.'

'Or she could be local. Someone who knows the area, knows Liffey Junction. None of the train guards saw her escaping with the freed prisoners. She melted away into the dark. So do your job, stay alert, and report back to me if you hear the faintest whisper. Understood?'

'Yes, sir.'

The German rose smoothly and walked off without a backward glance, leaving the envelope with Dennis's payment behind on the bench.

Dennis watched him go, relieved that the encounter was over. Then he slipped the money into his pocket, thought about what Vogts had said, and hoped that he could somehow satisfy the *Gestapo* man.

CHAPTER THIRTEEN

'It's a really weird feeling, isn't it?' said Mary as she walked with Roisin along the school corridor, the air heavy with the smell of floor polish.

'How do you mean?' asked Roisin.

They were making for the assembly hall in their convent school on this, the afternoon of the last day of term.

'Leaving it all behind,' said Mary. 'All the times we've given out about the nuns, and the rules, and teachers who annoyed us. But now that it's time to go, none of it seems so bad. I even feel I'm going to miss it. Is that mad?'

'No,' said Roisin, 'I think lots of the girls feel the same.'

They would be starting secondary school in September, and before that they had the whole summer to look forward to, but now Mary found herself looking backwards. She remembered her first day here as a Junior Infant, clinging to her mother's hand as they walked in through the school gates. She recalled her father smilingly admiring her outfit before she set off that morning, and she was suddenly hit by a sense of sadness. He wouldn't be there to wish her well when she started in her new secondary school, just as he hadn't been able to be there for any of the milestones in his children's lives over the past two years. She wished she could see him more often, though she knew she was luckier than the younger children in the family who thought he was dead. And she would see him soon, when Mam brought them all for their annual visit to her brother's farm outside Kinnitty, in County Offaly. Even though Dad would only visit secretly at night, Mary still counted the days until they would be together again.

'It'll probably be the same in our new school,' said Roisin, breaking her reverie.

'What will be the same?'

'We'll probably give out about it while we're there, and then feel sad when we're leaving. That's human nature, isn't it?'

'I suppose so,' answered Mary.

They reached the end of the corridor, then took their seats in the assembly hall. The room was filling up as sixth-year students from other classes arrived. Mary thought the atmosphere was a strange blend of giddiness and nostalgia, mixed with a curiosity about what Sister Regina, the principal, would say in her farewell address.

'Here's Queenie, now!' said Roisin, as Sister Regina swept into the hall.

She was a small woman, but she had an air of vigour about her, and all the girls rose to their feet when she entered the assembly hall.

The principal walked briskly through the hall and ascended the set of steps that led to the stage.

'You may be seated, girls,' she said in a strong voice that carried to all parts of the room.

'That's decent of her,' whispered Roisin playfully.

Mary knew better than to let the Sister Regina see her smiling, but she gave Roisin a quick wink, then sat down.

The principal waited until everyone was seated and the room was silent before speaking again. 'Good afternoon, girls.'

'Good afternoon, Sister.'

'This will be my final time to address you. Which may well come as a relief,' she added with a rare smile.

The girls dutifully laughed. Then Sister Regina's expression became serious again. 'You leave us here today, and we're sorry to see you go, but I wish you the very best in the next stage of your lives.'

Mary and Roisin exchanged a glance and Mary raised an eyebrow, as if to say that it wasn't very often that Queenie spoke so warmly.

Looking around the hall, the principal continued, her tone serious yet sympathetic. 'When you begin secondary school in September you'll be starting the move from childhood to adulthood. It will be an exciting time for you, but also a challenging and sometimes confusing time. We've tried here to instil in you Christian values, and when in doubt I would urge you to hold to those values. And that won't always be easy. We live in difficult times, when people with different values hold sway.'

Mary realised that the nun was referring to the Nazis. This was dangerous territory, and Mary glanced at Roisin. She could see that her friend was surprised by Sister Regina's approach, then the principal continued. 'Many people have had to make hard choices, many people have made difficult compromises with their consciences. In the coming years you too will have to make choices. When that day comes, ask yourselves: what's the right thing to do? What's the Christian thing to do? And pray for the strength to do that, come what may. Sometimes when things are bleak, it seems like the darkness will never lift. But in time it will, girls. In time the darkness *will* lift.'

Mary felt a stab of excitement. This was definitely a reference to the Nazi occupation, and she admired the principal's daring in raising the issue.

'Jesus promises in the gospel that the powers of darkness won't prevail against us,' said Regina. 'Good will triumph eventually. Meanwhile, here in Ireland, we mustn't despair – because good *will* win out in the end. And that's my message to you, girls, as you start the next phase of your lives. God bless you all.'

For a moment there was silence, then the room erupted into applause.

'Fair play to Queenie, I never knew she had it in her!' whispered Roisin.

'Me neither,' answered Mary as she applauded warmly.

Several girls at the front of the room rose to their feet, and within seconds the clapping had turned into a standing ovation.

Mary realised that most of the other pupils had also picked up on the principal's coded reference to the Nazis, and she felt a shiver go up her spine as the applause continued.

Sister Regina gave a bow of acknowledgement, and Mary could see that the nun was moved.

'Maybe there's hope for us yet,' said Roisin, indicating her applauding fellow pupils.

Mary had felt her spirits lifted too, and she nodded in agreement. 'Maybe there's hope for Ireland after all.'

CHAPTER FOURTEEN

Kevin knew he was being foolish. It was one thing taking risks to help the Resistance, but what he was about to do now wasn't Resistance work. And yet he felt that he had to strike some sort of blow. It was a balmy July evening, and the dusk was falling as he crouched behind a vehicle in the car park of Clontarf Golf Club, his opened penknife clutched in his hand.

Earlier in the day Dad had asked him to caddy for him, and normally Kevin liked the time they spent together on the golf course. Today, though, his father had agreed to play with Major Weber, and Kevin hated the idea of socialising for four hours with a Nazi. He understood Dad's point that to refuse Webber's invitation would seem like an insult. And he, in turn, couldn't insult Dad by refusing to caddy for him.

Normally he could have claimed that he had something planned with his friends, but Mary was away in Kinnitty, and Roisin and her aunt were gone into town. Because of the warm weather Kevin had planned to swim in the canal with some of the other boys and girls from the area. But that was the kind of casual arrangement that anyone could drop in and out of, and not a strong enough reason to say no to his father's request.

Kevin had decided instead to make the best of it, and he had tried to be upbeat as he drove with his father to the golf club. Major Weber had been his usual smarmy self, but what had really depressed Kevin was the arrival of the third golfer in their group. Webber introduced his colleague as *Kriminalkommisar* Heinrich Vogts, and Kevin realised that this was the *Gestapo* officer who had questioned Roisin and Mary. *And quite possibly had chosen Sean Murray for execution as part of the reprisals.*

Vogts and Weber were both skilful players, and from a golfing point of view the game had gone well. Socially too his father had got on with the Germans, but without being too subservient. But Kevin resented the two men behaving as though this was their club, and he hated the dismissive way Weber had talked down to the middle-aged caddy he had hired. And Vogts had refused to have a caddy, instead exuding the air of a man supremely confident of his own judgement and ability.

Last night, though, Kevin had heard on *Radio Freedom* that the Germans and Russians had clashed at a place called Kursk, in the biggest tank battle in history. According to the radio, the Nazis had suffered a major set-back, but Vogts and Weber still behaved with the arrogance of men for whom defeat seemed unthinkable.

The idea spurred Kevin into action now. He gripped the pen-knife tightly and pushed the tip of the blade into the tyre nozzle of the car at whose side he was crouched. It was the gleaming black Daimler in which Vogts had arrived, and Kevin heard a satisfying hiss as the air escaped. He knew that deflating the *Gestapo* man's tyre was only a gesture, and maybe a childish one, at that. But the

Gestapo were bullying thugs, and Kevin resented the way they had terrified so many girls in Phibsboro with their questioning after the Liffey Junction raid. *So let Kriminalkommissar Vogts work up a sweat loosening the wheel bolts and jacking up his precious Daimler to change the tyre.*

Just then Kevin heard the sound of footsteps and he immediately removed the knife. The hissing stopped, and Kevin froze, his heart racing madly. He heard two men speaking in German, but to his relief they weren't Weber and Vogts. Still, if either of them walked down the line of cars, he would be spotted. Kevin waited, not daring to move a muscle. He had told Dad that he was going out to the toilet, and if he was gone too long it would seem odd. But he couldn't suddenly stand up now and walk out from behind the cars.

He waited impatiently as the two men engaged in a protracted farewell. Eventually there was the sound of car doors being slammed and engines being started. Kevin felt a surge of relief when the cars drove off. He knew he had had a near miss, but before he lost his nerve he stuck the penknife into the nozzle again and released the rest of the air from the tyre. Still gripping the knife, he paused briefly. He was tempted to damage the Daimler's gleaming paintwork by carving on it the hated Nazi symbol, the swastika. *No,* he told himself, *don't push your luck.* The puncture could appear to be an accident, but Vogts would know it was a deliberate act of resistance if a *Gestapo* vehicle was damaged.

Instead Kevin closed the blade of the knife and slipped it into his pocket. He rose, dusted off his knees, and looked around. The car park was still empty. Moving smartly, but trying to appear casual, he made his way back towards the clubhouse.

Mary reckoned that she must have the strangest summer holidays of any girl in Ireland, as she sat at her uncle's kitchen table. Not that she was complaining; many people couldn't afford *any* holidays. Though at the other extreme wealthy people and black marketeers could stay in upmarket country hotels where – despite the strict rationing in the cities – good food was generally available. But nobody except Mary went on holidays with a widowed mother whose husband secretly visited them every night.

Mary was the eldest child, with her seven-year-old sister Gretta next in line, followed by the five-year-old twins Sean and Deirdre. It wouldn't be possible to fool Gretta for much longer, Mary felt, but for now her father's presence was still a secret, and Dad visited Mary and her mother late at night when the younger children were asleep.

Mary loved their annual visit to her mother's home place, with the farm now run by Mam's brother, Uncle Brendan. Brendan was soft-spoken and quiet, but although a bachelor himself, he liked children and he allowed Mary, Gretta, and the twins the run of the farm. More importantly he was staunchly anti-Nazi, and he happily went along with Mary's father visiting the remote farm each night under cover of darkness. The farmhouse itself was a large rambling building with outhouses attached, and Mary knew that Dad slipped away early each morning, back to the Resistance camps in the nearby Slieve Bloom mountains.

She also knew that the Slieve Blooms was where some of the freed prisoners from the train rescue were hiding. Even now, two weeks after the rescue operation, she still felt proud at playing a role and then keeping her nerve when questioned by the Germans. For the last few days, however, there had been no discussion of the war, or the Resistance, and everyone had just unwound and savoured the holiday.

Mary had played camogie with cousins who lived near Birr, and had practised her tin whistle, teaching herself how to play 'Whispering Grass', the Inkspots song that Mam loved.

Mam had been much more carefree than usual over the last few days, and Mary thought it was lovely to see how happy her parents were on these precious nights that they could spend together. She made sure to give them as much time together as possible, but for now all three of them were relaxed as they sat at the kitchen table. The room felt cosy, softly lit by a couple of lamps, and Mary's mother looked up enquiringly

'Will we finish up with a cup of tea?' she asked. 'It's going to get chilly.'

Normally Mam was careful with the tea ration, and Mary was touched that her mother had saved her tea so that there would be no shortage during the special time when Dad was with them.

'Why not?' said her father. 'Sure we'll be a long time dead!'

'Talking of chilly, Mam, what do you get if you cross a snowman and a vampire?'

'I just know this will be daft,' said Mam, 'but go on, what do you get?'

'Frostbite!'

Everyone laughed, and Dad entered into the spirit of things by raising his hand like a pupil in school. 'I've a question,' he said. 'What building in New York has the most stories?'

'Eh...the Empire State Building?' answered Mary.

'Any other answers?'

'The Chrysler Building?' suggested Mam.

'Sorry, you're both wrong. It's the New York Public Library.'

'Really?' said Mary.

'The most *stories*? In the *library*?' said her father laughingly.

'Ah, Dad, that's a trick question!'

'But a good one.'

'Only if you're a smart Alec,' said Mam playfully. 'I'm going to make that tea.'

She left the room and went out to the scullery, where Mary could hear her filling a kettle.

'So,' said Dad, 'enjoying the holiday?'

'It's lovely, Dad. Especially...'

'Especially, what?'

'Seeing you every night. I...I miss you.'

'I miss you too, love. I miss all of you. You've no idea how much.'

Mary swallowed hard. She felt a welling up of affection for her father and she reached out and squeezed his hand. Wordlessly he squeezed back. Then, after a moment, he seemed to gather himself. 'But it won't be forever, Mary. It won't be forever.'

She looked at him quizzically. 'Is there…is there something planned?'

Her father hesitated. 'I shouldn't really be talking about this.'

'Come on, Dad! I know normally you have to be on guard. But you can trust your family.'

'I know that, pet. You've been a rock.'

'Then talk to me.'

Her father hesitated again, then spoke softly. 'The Resistance has been involved in a big intelligence-gathering operation.'

'Yes?'

'To beat the Nazis, the Allies must invade Europe. And Ireland's the most westerly country in Europe. There are radar stations along the west coast and naval bases too.'

'Right.'

'So it's no secret that the Allies will land forces here. The question the Germans have to worry about is where?'

'And how does the Resistance come into it?'

'We've identified landing sites for the Allies. And we're drawing up really detailed reports on German forces and where they're deployed. Airfields, naval bases, fuel dumps, troop concentrations, where armour and artillery are located. That kind of information can be the difference between victory and defeat when the Allies land.'

'Yes.'

'We've got maps, photographs, drawings – stuff that has to go to Allied Command in Iceland. And that…that brings me to something you won't like.'

'What?' said Mary, unable to keep the worry from her voice.

'I hadn't planned to tell you this till the holiday was over, but now that it's come up, I won't mislead you. I'll…I'll have to go to Iceland myself.'

'To Iceland?! But…how would you even get there?'

'A submarine will be sent in a few weeks' time, when all the reports are finished.'

'But…why does it have to be you who goes?'

'This is vital information, Mary. I need to go through it in detail with the right people in Iceland.'

'And how long would you be gone for?'

Her father shrugged. 'I don't know, exactly.'

'So when will we see you again?'

'You'll see me every day for the rest of the holiday. And when you're in summer camp I promise I'll get to see you somehow before I leave.'

'OK. But…when you go to Iceland…you don't know how long you'll be there for?'

'No. But the Resistance work is crucial. So I'm hoping they'll want me back in Ireland.'

'You're *hoping*?'

'I'm *confident* they'll want me back in Ireland.'

'So what, you'll come back in another submarine?'

'Maybe, if they can spare one. Or they might parachute me back in.'

'But you've never parachuted in your life, Dad!'

'Neither has anyone, until the first time they parachute.'

'Even so…'

Her father took her hand. 'Try not to worry, Mary. Every day since the Germans landed has meant *some* danger. But they haven't caught me yet, and I've no plans to fall into their hands.'

'Now, here we are,' said Mam, entering the room with tea and apple tart on a tray. 'Your favourite, Mary,' said her mother indicating the apple tart.

'Thanks, Mam.'

'Meanwhile, we'll take things a day at a time, and enjoy the rest of the holiday,' said Dad. 'All right?'

'All right,' answered Mary as cheerfully as she could. Then she sipped her tea and ate the tart, trying hard to put her worries aside, and to savour every minute of the time left with her father.

CHAPTER FIFTEEN

oisin cycled along King Street, pleased that her efforts had paid off. It was an uphill cycle home to Phibsboro from Stoneybatter but she didn't care. Muldoon's fish shop in King Street sometimes acquired fresh pike, alongside more popular fish like cod and haddock, and this afternoon Roisin had used her ration coupons to buy a portion of pike.

Once home she would mince it and mix it with egg, onions and bread to make Gefilte fish, a traditional Jewish dish that her mother had taught her how to prepare. Roisin wasn't a practising Jew, and had been brought up a Catholic, but she felt that keeping some Jewish practices was a link to her mother.

The Nazis had made any Jewish allegiance extremely dangerous, but Roisin was determined not to be cowed by them. Although her mother had never been strongly religious, she had maintained the tradition of cooking a special meal on Friday evening, the eve of Sabbath. Roisin remembered with affection the tasty meals of Gefilte fish that the family had had in Cork before the war and, despite Aunt Nuala's kindness, hardly a day went by when she didn't miss her mother, with her winning smile and her quirky sense of humour.

Rising in the saddle now and turning left at the junction of Constitution Hill, Roisin began the long climb towards Phibsboro. The memory of Friday night meals was a bittersweet one, triggering thoughts of her parents, and making her wonder how they were. Although conditions were harsh in Spike Island Concentration Camp, Roisin knew that her mother was alive. But Dad – big, strong, Dad who made her feel safe and who could always make her laugh – how was he? Had he been worked half to death in the labour camp in Germany? Was he even still alive?

No, she decided, if she dwelt on her worries she would give way to despair. Every day she prayed for both her parents, and she had done so today too. That was all she could do for now, and so she forced herself not to fret about it any further.

The late afternoon sun was hazy, and Roisin was glad not to be making her way up Constitution Hill in hot sunshine. As she cycled, Broadstone Railway Station loomed ahead on her left, a large swastika flag hanging at the station entrance, while across the road the trees in the grounds of the King's Inns law complex swayed in a light summer breeze.

Suddenly Roisin's attention was caught by the sight of a familiar figure. Walking down the far side of the road and approaching the entrance to King's Inns, was Dennis O'Sullivan. He hadn't seen Roisin, but she was struck by his demeanour. Just before he entered the grounds of the King's Inns he glanced around, as if to make sure he wasn't being followed. It was only a small gesture, but something about it made Roisin halt. What was he up to?

Dennis walked on at a leisurely pace. Acting on instinct, Roisin dismounted and crossed the road, wanting to keep him in sight.

There were children playing on the grass, people sitting on benches, and babies being wheeled in prams, but Roisin kept her eyes focused on Dennis.

She pretended to adjust the chain of her bicycle as she watched him approaching a bench. A man was sitting on the bench reading a newspaper, and Dennis sat down near him. Something about the arrangement seemed unnatural to Roisin, but nothing prepared her for the shock when the man turned a page of his newspaper and his face became visible. It was Vogts, the *Gestapo* officer who had come for her in Cork, and who had questioned Mary in St Peter's School

Roisin felt her blood run cold, and she stood unmoving as a horrible notion struck her. *Dennis O'Sullivan was a collaborator.* Even though she really disliked him, she didn't want it to be true. But as he sat there, Roisin could see that he was talking quietly. After a few moments Dennis rose, and Roisin saw him discreetly slip an envelope into his pocket. *That settled it,* she thought with horror. There was no other explanation. Dennis O'Sullivan was working for the *Gestapo* as a paid informer.

She turned away, her thoughts in turmoil as she mounted her bicycle, crossed the road, and cycled for home.

The bright red raspberry flavouring nestled on top of the Knicker-erbocker Glory and, lazily wielding a long-handled spoon, Dennis

scooped it up with melting ice cream and transferred it to his mouth. He savoured the cool, sweet taste, then treated himself to another spoonful, swirling the delicious mixture around his tongue.

It was Saturday afternoon, and he was seated in a café in O'Connell Street. He wondered idly if the café owner supplemented his precious supply of ice cream and syrup on the black market. Or maybe the owner had won favour with the Germans by actively collaborating. Not that Dennis cared. He had ordered the most expensive ice cream on the menu, happy in the knowledge that he could afford such luxury. Up to now he had been saving the weekly fee he got from *Kriminalkommissar* Vogts, and it was mounting up nicely towards the motorbike that he wanted to buy when he was old enough. Today though he had felt like splurging, and so he had taken the bus into town and gone to the fancy café.

Eating his ice cream now in leisurely fashion, he thought back over the last few months with satisfaction. Vogts was a demanding boss, but he always paid up, even on weeks when Dennis didn't have much information to pass on. And it was good to be associated with a man of real power, who wasn't afraid to take action. Within a week of Dennis telling Vogts about Father Graham and his anti-German sermon, the cocky young priest had arrived home one night with a black eye, a split lip, and all the swagger gone from his demeanour. Dennis had never liked Father Graham, and thought that he had gotten off lightly with a hiding when he could have ended up in a concentration camp. Although it was never officially acknowledged that the priest had received his injuries from the *Gestapo*, Dennis found it exciting to realise that he had indirectly wielded the power that lead to Graham being taught a lesson.

The hunt for the girl involved in the Liffey Junction raid had been less successful and despite Vogts putting him under pressure, Dennis had been unable to provide any clues to her identity. Still, Vogts would be pleased that only yesterday two more escaped prisoners had been caught in Limerick. Both had been reported as 'shot while trying to escape', which everyone knew meant they had been executed.

Lots of Irish people were up in arms about that, but Dennis could see the *Gestapo* reasoning. As far as the Nazis were concerned these were the enemy, so what was the difference between killing them on the battle field or killing them after they had taken part in an escape bid? As Da said, the Germans were in charge, and the smart thing was not to oppose them.

Thinking now about the rest of the summer, Dennis was looking forward to the youth club holiday in Galway, and he was glad that he hadn't reported Mr Cox regarding the black armbands. Instead Mr Cox had received the necessary permit from the authorities, and the camp would be starting in two weeks' time.

The holiday was reasonably priced, and this year Dennis would have plenty of spending money while at camp. In addition to what he got from *Kriminalkommissar* Vogts he had a summer job delivering newspapers every weekend. It was an easy job, and apart from the cash, Dennis found it a useful way to meet people when delivering their newspapers. Customers often chatted, and Dennis was always delighted when he got paid on the double, both for doing the deliveries and for reporting to Vogts information that his customers let slip.

He finished the Knickerbocker Glory, then paused. He had never been in the café before, only seeing it from the outside. *Well, he was on the inside now. And that's the way he planned to keep it.* Pleased with the thought, and feeling like a man of means, he sat back in his chair, signalled for the waitress, and ordered himself another Knickerbocker Glory.

The Sunday Mass bells pealed out, the bright July sun shone on the sparkling water of the canal, and there was a peaceful stillness in the summer air. But Kevin was agitated and had lowered his fishing road onto the bank.

'I don't believe it!' he said.

'Believe it,' answered Roisin, 'it's true.'

She sat beside him on the bank of the Royal Canal. 'I wanted to tell you on Friday night or yesterday, but I couldn't find you.'

'We were visiting relations,' said Kevin absent-mindedly.

'Right.'

'God!' said Kevin, shaking his head. 'It's…it's disgusting. How could anyone stoop so low?' He had despised Dennis O'Sullivan as a bully and a braggart, but to hear that he was also a paid informer was a shock.

'Some people only care about themselves,' said Roisin.

'But to sell out your own country? Your own people? People you may have known for years?'

'It's horrible all right. But we need to handle it very carefully'

'Yes. Sorry, my head is still spinning,' said Kevin. 'You've had time to think it over. What do you feel we should do?'

'We have to be even more careful now when he's around. We also need to let the Resistance know he's spying.'

'Right.' Kevin knew that the battle between the Resistance and the *Gestapo* was a nasty one. The *Gestapo* were murdering thugs. The Resistance could be ruthless too when it came to dealing with traitors, and that raised a worrying thought. 'I hate Dennis O'Sullivan,' he said, 'but...would we be putting his life in danger?'

'He's the one who did that by spying for the Nazis,' said Roisin. 'How many Irish lives has he put in danger?'

'True.'

'Even so, I doubt that the Resistance would kill a kid.'

'I don't want him shot,' said Kevin. 'But I can't bear to see him get away with it either. Maybe we could pay him back in a smarter way?'

'How do you mean?'

'Supposing we could find a way to feed him false information? Mary could talk to her dad about it. It would kill two birds with one stone if the Germans were misled, and then it backfired on Dennis for misleading them.'

'I don't know. Sounds pretty complicated.'

'But it would really teach him a lesson if the Nazis rounded on him.'

'Let's be careful, Kevin. I can't stand Dennis O'Sullivan, and I know he's been horrible to you. Getting revenge on him, it's not as important as protecting our own lives.' Roisin looked him in the eye. 'OK?'

'OK.'

'I mean it, Kevin.'

'I know.'

'Be sure you do. Really, he's not worth it.'

Kevin could see the concern in his friend's eyes and he nodded reassuringly. 'Don't worry, I won't do anything stupid.' And he wouldn't, he thought, recognising that Roisin was right about safeguarding their own lives. But Dennis O'Sullivan had crossed a line. And, although Kevin didn't know how he would do it, somehow he had to pay him back.

CHAPTER SIXTEEN

Mary hated goodbyes, but she was determined not to cry. She knew it was hard enough for her father living on the run, and away from his family, without adding to his problems with a tearful farewell. They were in the softly-lit kitchen of Uncle Brendan's farmhouse on this, Dad's last night with them, and she suspected that Mam had deliberately absented herself to the scullery to give her and Dad some final time together.

That afternoon Mary had done something similar when she had taken the younger children in the family on a walk, knowing that Dad was planning a rare daytime appearance at the farm. For their last day together Mam and Dad had secretly gone swimming at a remote spot on the Camcor River, and now with her siblings asleep in bed Mary was having her last moments of the holiday with her father.

'It's been good spending time together,' said Dad, placing his hand affectionately on her shoulder. 'Really good.'

Mary nodded. 'Yes, it was brilliant.' She hesitated, then looked him in the eye. 'I…I have to ask, Dad. Must it really be you who goes to Iceland?'

Dad reached down and took her hand. 'I know it's hard to accept, love,' he said gently. 'I'm sure most girls your age have their fathers at home. But I've got to deliver this information. The war is on a knife edge. The Allied invasion of Ireland *has* to succeed, otherwise…'

'Otherwise what?'

'Otherwise the Nazis continue to rule. If it wasn't for the Russians they'd already be complete masters of Europe.'

'But aren't they losing to the Russians now?'

Her father nodded. 'The Red Army's won big battles on the Eastern Front. But at a terrible cost. And there's no guarantee they'll go on winning. We can't keep asking them to bear the brunt of fighting the Nazis. As their allies, we *have* to launch an invasion here in the West.'

'It's all so crazy. The Red Army used to be on the same side as the Nazis.'

'Wars are rarely simple, Mary. It's true the Russians and the Nazis agreed to split Poland between them, but that was early in the war. When Hitler invaded Russia everything changed, and we ended up on the same side.'

'But they're not really our friends, then, are they? They're just fighting the Germans because they were invaded.'

'True. But Norway, and Belgium, and Holland were all neutral – until *they* were invaded. So were we, for that matter. Countries do what's in their own interest.'

'Right.'

'I have to deliver this key intelligence. But I give you my word, I'll do everything in my power to get back to Ireland as quickly as I can. Is that fair enough?'

'OK, Dad.'

'And…I shouldn't really be saying this. But the submarine that comes for me will surface off the Galway coast. So I'll be in that part of the country when you're on summer camp. Like I said, I promise I'll try and see you before I leave. All right?'

'All right, Dad. And…and if you can't…that's OK too, I understand.'

Her father looked at her, and she saw him swallowing hard.

'You're…you're a great girl, Mary,' he said, his voice heavy with emotion. 'I don't know what I did to deserve you.' Without another word he opened his arms.

Mary stepped forward immediately and wrapped herself in his embrace. She felt her eyes welling up with tears, but she remembered her promise to herself not to cry and make things harder for Dad. Instead she buried her head in his shoulder, kept her eyes shut and hugged him tightly.

Roisin felt a little uneasy as Dennis O'Sullivan drew near. She had cut down the laneway behind the soccer stadium at Dalymount Park, taking a short cut to the North Circular Road. Dennis was coming in the opposite direction down the narrow laneway, the afternoon air dusty in the July heat, and he smirked as he drew near.

The fact that he was reporting to the *Gestapo* made him dangerous now as well as being a bully, but Roisin kept her face impassive.

'All on your owneo?' he said, standing in her way. 'You don't normally go anywhere without your little gang.'

'I have friends, not a gang.'

'Is that so?'

'I don't need a gang,' said Roisin. 'I can stand on my own two feet.'

'I don't think, though, that your wishy-washy friend can, do you?'

Roisin knew that Dennis was referring to Kevin, but she wasn't going to give him the satisfaction of a response.

'Not going to defend him?

'I don't need to defend my friends to you.'

'That's where you're wrong. Burke always needs support. Weeds like him haven't the guts to stand up for themselves.'

'I bet he wishes he was a big, brave, tough guy like you,' said Roisin sarcastically. She could see that Dennis was irritated by her response, and when he spoke now there was more venom in his voice.

'I'll tell you what he'll wish. He'll wish he didn't leave his mammy and daddy behind and go to summer camp. We'll have loads of time together over in Galway. I'd say I'll definitely bump into him when he's on his own. Guess what's going to happen then?'

'Nothing's going to happen then.'

'Wrong. Plenty's going to happen.'

Roisin looked him in the eye. 'Why are you being like this?'

'Because you all think you're so smart. Well, we'll see how smart you feel when I make Burke's life a misery!'

'You won't get away with that.'

'Who'll stop me?'

'I will.'

'How are you going to do that?' asked Dennis aggressively. He drew nearer till his face was just inches from Roisin's. 'How are you going to stop me, smart Alec?!'

Roisin's patience snapped. 'I'll tell people you're a traitor!' she said. Dennis's stance had brought him so close that she could smell his breath, but instead of drawing away she drew even nearer. 'I'll tell them you're an informer who takes money from the *Gestapo*! That's how I'll stop you!'

Dennis pulled back, and Roisin could see that he was badly shocked.

'I saw you in the King's Inns. You're just a snivelling little collaborator,' she added. 'And if you so much as look crooked at Kevin, I'll make sure everyone knows it.'

Dennis stood unmoving, and Roisin couldn't help but take pleasure at seeing a bully rendered speechless. She knew she had been impetuous in showing her hand like this. She and Kevin had agreed to act cautiously regarding Dennis's role as a collaborator, but they hadn't known this situation would arise, and Roisin wasn't sorry that she had used the information to stop Dennis in his tracks.

He still had said nothing, and she could see that he was trying to come up with a response.

'Don't bother denying it,' she said. 'I saw you being paid by Vogts.'

Dennis looked thoughtful, then eventually looked up and meet her gaze.

'Who's denying it?' he said.

Roisin was taken aback. She had expected bluster or some kind of half-baked explanation. Instead Dennis repeated his question, his voice becoming more assured. 'Who's denying it? Did you think I was going to quake in my boots in case you told people?'

'You'd be wise to quake in your boots,' answered Roisin. 'Collaborators don't do well.'

'Only if people *know* they're collaborators. But I don't need to deny it to you, because you're not going to spread the word.'

Roisin was thrown by his confidence, but she kept her voice sceptical. 'Really?'

'Yes, really. If you open your mouth, you'll be arrested. I'll tell Vogts I think you're the girl they've been searching for, the one who stopped the train.'

'You haven't a shred of proof. I'd nothing to do with stopping any train.'

'I'll say I heard rumours. Vogts is mad keen to get his hands on this mystery girl. You'll be in a *Gestapo* cell before you know it. And it won't be questioning like the day in the school. It will be full *Gestapo* interrogation.'

Despite the warmth of summer, Roisin felt a shiver run up her spine, but tried not to show her fear.

'So keep your mouth shut tight,' said Dennis. 'If even one person says the word informer to me, you'll end up in a cell screaming for your precious auntie.'

Roisin didn't know what to say, and before she could think of a response Dennis pointed a finger aggressively at her.

'Don't say you haven't been warned!'

He walked past her, and Roisin stood unmoving in the lane, her heart thumping, as she tried to absorb what had just happened.

CHAPTER SEVENTEEN

Kevin crunched a piece of candy-striped rock, its sweet, chewy centre sticking agreeably to his teeth. Mary had given her friends small bars of rock with the word Birr running through them now that she had returned from her holiday in County Offaly.

It was a showery July evening, and with heavy rain having fallen all day, Kevin had spent the afternoon sketching and reading. Tonight, though, he had invited Roisin and Mary to come to his house and catch up on all the news. They were seated in the parlour, but although Kevin loved the sweet taste of rock, he was chewing automatically, his mind elsewhere since Roisin had told her alarming story about Dennis O'Sullivan.

His initial reaction had been unease when he heard that Dennis planned to pick on him at their isolated campsite in County Galway. His own concerns had swiftly receded, however, when he had heard of Roisin being threatened with arrest by the *Gestapo*.

'I'm dead grateful that you stood up for me, Roisin,' he said. 'But I wish you hadn't put yourself in danger.'

'Well, it can't be undone now. But I've been thinking about it,' she added. 'It's probably just an empty threat.'

'Why do you think that?' asked Mary.

'Because when I had him on the ropes about being an informer he was desperate. And this was what he came up with. So I'd say it's just a threat to shut me up.'

'I really hope you're right,' said Kevin.

'He must know, too, that if I was arrested people would hear that he'd caused it,' said Roisin. 'He'd be despised, and completely boycotted by everyone around here. He'd hate that.'

Kevin thought this was a fair point, and he wanted to believe it would protect his friend. But he still felt they had to be cautious. 'Probably the safest thing, though, is to do what he said and keep the information to yourself.'

'Absolutely,' said Roisin. 'I'm not trying to be a hero here. It's terrifying to think of being taken in by the *Gestapo*. And if they found out my mam is Jewish….'

'I know,' said Mary. 'You can't do anything that risks that.'

'Well, except there's one thing that has to be done.'

'What's that?' asked Kevin.

'The Resistance have to be told,' said Roisin. 'We can't have a German informer watching everything that happens around here and not tip them off.'

Kevin could see the logic of this, but his worry must have shown because Roisin raised a hand before he could speak. 'It can be done discreetly, explaining my position. Mary, you could get word to your dad, so they know what Dennis is up to.'

'Sure.'

'And your dad can make certain it doesn't get out, and the Resistance don't do anything that puts me at risk,' added Roisin.

'That won't be a problem,' said Mary. 'Right now the Resistance don't want to do anything that will bring more of a spotlight on them.'

'Because of the train rescue?' asked Kevin.

Mary shook her head. 'Not just that.'

'What then?' asked Roisin.

Mary hesitated. 'I'm not really supposed to talk about it. But... there's an important operation going on. Something that's vital for the future. So the last thing the Resistance wants in the next few weeks is any extra attention.'

'Fine,' said Roisin.

'So apart from telling Dad, do we leave it as a stand-off with Dennis?' asked Mary. 'If he says nothing further, we say nothing further. What do you think?'

'It's probably the best we can do for now,' said Roisin.

'Kevin?' asked Mary

Kevin hated the idea of Dennis O'Sullivan getting away with being a traitor, but he couldn't see any alternative. 'OK,' he said, 'let's go with that.'

'All right,' said Mary. 'Now, let's forget Dennis O'Sullivan, have some more rock, and catch up on all the news.'

Kevin still felt uneasy, but hid it for the sake of his friends. 'More rock is always good,' he said cheerfully. Then he broke off another piece, smiled at the girls, and popped the rock into his mouth.

'Have a good look at that!' said Aunt Nuala. 'What do you think that is?!'

'A…a packed suitcase,' answered Roisin, shaken to see her normally good-humoured aunt so angry. They were in Nuala's neatly laid out bedroom, and her aunt had pulled the suitcase from the back of the wardrobe, chucked it onto the bed and opened it.

'And what do you think it's for?' demanded Nuala.

'Your…your holidays?'

'No, Roisin, it's not for my holidays! It's ready in case we have to flee at a moment's notice! And you've brought that closer with your reckless behaviour!'

In the couple of days since her encounter with Dennis O'Sullivan, Roisin had agonised over whether or not to tell Aunt Nuala what had happened. In the end she had felt that it was only fair to warn her that Dennis had threatened to involve the *Gestapo*.

'I'm really sorry,' she said now. 'I was just trying to protect Kevin.'

'You didn't think it through! In protecting Kevin, you've put us at real risk.'

'I honestly don't think Dennis will follow through on his threat.'

'You can't know that.'

'But I know Dennis. He's not going to want people to hear that he's a collaborator. If I was arrested, everyone in Phibsboro would know he was an informer.'

'*If you were arrested?!* Are you listening to yourself? It was incredibly reckless to confront him.'

'I can see that now. And…'

176

'And what?'

'After all you've done for me, I'm so, so sorry for causing more trouble.' She looked at her aunt, whose expression softened a little.

'It's just that…I really hate bullies, and he was bullying my friend. I'm sorry for putting us at risk, but…but that's why I did it.'

Aunt Nuala didn't reply at once, and when she did her tone was more sympathetic. 'I hate bullies too. But Kevin being bullied is one thing. Us being *executed* is another. If they ever find out who you are, and what I did, we'll end up dead. I thought you understood that.'

'I do, but…'

'There's no buts. We can't afford needless risks. And this was a needless risk.'

Roisin found it hard to meet her aunt's gaze. She had come this far, though, and she decided to be completely honest now. 'It…it wasn't just Kevin that made me do it.'

'Oh? What else was it?'

'It's…it's Mam and Dad,' she said softly.

'How do you mean?' asked Nuala.

Roisin looked her aunt in the eye. 'You've been so good to me. I could never thank you enough. But…but sometimes I still really miss Mam and Dad.'

'Of course you do, love. That's only natural.'

'And even though I pray every day, I still worry about what will happen them. We don't even know if Dad is still alive.' Rosin could feel tears forming in her eyes but she carried on. 'I've tried really hard to be brave, but…I know this is stupid, but…'

'But what, love?

'Part of threatening Dennis O'Sullivan was trying to fight back. The Nazis have ruined everything. They've taken my mam and my dad.' The tears were rolling down her cheeks now but she didn't care. 'They've taken Mam and Dad and…something inside me snapped, and I just wanted to strike back.'

Roisin wiped her eyes and when she looked again at Nuala she saw that she too was tearful.

'Come here, love,' her aunt said, opening her arms.

Roisin moved to her, and Nuala hugged her.

'You're not angry at me then?' said Roisin.

'No pet, what's done is done. And don't you worry. Whatever happens, we'll face it together.'

Roisin felt a flood of relief, and despite her best efforts she was wracked with sobs.

'Just let it all out, darling,' said Nuala, 'You've kept it bottled up for long enough. Just let it all out.'

Roisin gripped her aunt tightly, and for the first time in a long while, cried floods of tears for all that she had lost.

CHAPTER EIGHTEEN

ennis didn't like graveyards, but for tonight's meeting with *Kriminalkommissar* Vogts he had been instructed to visit Glasnevin Cemetery again. Dennis went in the main entrance, the tall column of the O'Connell Monument bathed in hazy evening sunshine as he walked past it on his way to a remote section of the graveyard bordering the rear of the Botanic Gardens.

Despite the cemetery giving him the creeps, he felt that it was a better meeting place than the more public King's Inns grounds, where Roisin Tierney had seen him with Vogts. For some reason the German had switched their meeting that week to Friday afternoon, and Dennis had silently cursed the *Gestapo* man for changing from their usual Sunday evening rendezvous.

The threat to Roisin to keep her mouth shut seemed to have worked, however, which was a big relief. Yet it raised a question. For Roisin not to reveal his role as a collaborator *after* he threatened her with the *Gestapo* made sense. But why had she done nothing *before* his threat? Five days had elapsed between the meeting in King's Inns and his encounter with Roisin in the laneway at Dalymount Park. Clearly, she disliked him, and could have been expected to enjoy unmasking him. Yet she had chosen not to reveal his secret. Why? Could it be that she didn't want the attention that would come with unmasking him? Maybe she had something of her own to hide – lots of people had done things during the occupation that they didn't want revealed. And if there *was* anything untoward on her record it would be well worth knowing.

Preoccupied with his thoughts, Dennis walked on through the cemetery, growing a little uneasy now, as he always was when meeting Vogts. He had decided that he wouldn't tell the Nazi that his cover was blown – that might end his role, with its welcome weekly payment. But he could casually mention Roisin's name among some other information, and suggest checking her file. Perhaps claim that there were rumours she was engaged in anti-Nazi talk. Or he could say nothing for now. It would probably be best to play it by ear, he decided, with his approach depending on the German's mood.

He turned a corner and saw Vogts up ahead, sitting on a bench beneath a mature oak tree.

Dennis approached him, and with nobody in sight, the *Gestapo* man dispensed with the pretence of reading his newspaper. He gave a curt nod, then looked enquiringly at Dennis.

'Make your report.'

Dennis gathered himself, then he sat down on the bench and began to speak.

'When are we going to tell the truth, Mam?' asked Mary. It was Sunday afternoon, and her younger siblings were playing outside while she had stayed back in the kitchen to help her mother prepare dinner. Mam was good at stretching out their rations, and with even a small portion of chicken she could make a tasty casserole, but today Mary had more grave concerns than food. 'Gretta's seven now,' she said, 'and it's going to get harder to fool her about Dad.'

Mam put down the casserole dish that was in her hands and indicated the kitchen table.

'Sit down, love.'

Mary did as her mother suggested, and when they were both seated Mam reached out and took her hand.

'I understand you don't like lying, Mary. I hate it too. But we can't tell the others yet.'

'It's just—'

'Mary,' said Mam, cutting her off. 'Think this through. What could happen if Gretta had known Dad was alive, and she'd let something slip on the street? None of us knew Dennis O'Sullivan was an informer. Supposing he'd heard her?'

'I know…' conceded Mary.

'We've taken huge risks as a family, and I've gone along,' said Mam. 'We're all in this to free Ireland. But Gretta's just seven, and Deirdre and Sean are five. They *have* to be kept in the dark.'

'I understand, Mam, it's just…it's bad enough always being on guard against the Germans. But having to watch what you say in front of your own brothers and sisters…'

Her mother squeezed her hand. 'It won't be forever, love. This time next year the Allies could have freed us.'

'I'm living for that day,' said Mary. 'Though Dad says a lot of things have to go right for the invasion to succeed.'

'They do. But Dad is determined to make that happen. That's why he has to go to Iceland.'

'Right.'

'It's really hard for Dad, living in the shadows. And now he has this vital mission. Our job is to not give him anything more to worry about. All right?'

'All right, Mam.'

Mary thought her mother's attitude was amazing. For the last two years she had single-handedly raised four children while only occasionally seeing her husband. She had risked arrest, and interrogation, and never once complained. And in spite of carrying that burden, her main concern now was not to give Dad any additional worries.

'I've…I've never said this, Mam,' said Mary, struggling to put her feelings into words. 'But…but the way you handle it all…I think you're brilliant.'

Her mother's face lit up, and Mary thought how much younger she looked when she smiled.

'Thanks, chicken,' said Mam softly. 'You're not too bad yourself!'

It was typical of her mother to make light of a compliment, Mary thought. Still though, she could see that what she had said had affected Mam, and she was glad that she had spoken up.

'And I hope you've a great time at the camp next week, love,' added her mother.

'I'm sure we will.'

'But be careful. With Dennis O'Sullivan there you have to be extra cautious. Dad is determined to see you one last time before he goes. You need to make absolutely certain the two of them don't cross paths.'

'Don't worry, Mam. When it comes to Dennis O'Sullivan – I'll be watching his every move.'

Kevin thought that religion could sometimes be strange, as he tucked into his dinner. Being Catholics, the Burkes were forbidden to eat meat on a Friday, and Father Graham had explained that this was in atonement for the sins of the world. Most people in Dublin therefore ate fish on Friday, but Kevin found it hard to see how this was a penance. In fact, his Friday dinner of fish and chips was his favourite meal of the week, and Roisin and Mary had laughed out loud at a cartoon he had drawn of himself scoffing a plate of fish and chips while Father Graham looked disconcerted in the background.

He was seated now at the kitchen table with his parents, enjoying a long ray covered in batter, and savouring soft, mushy chips that had been doused in vinegar.

'I've a joke for you, Kevin,' said his mother looking at him good humouredly.

Mam might be a good violinist but she wasn't good at telling jokes. Kevin knew, though, that she was in high spirits because her bridge team had won an important match this morning, and he smiled at her. 'What is it?'

'What did the fish say when he got out on bail?'

'What did he say?'

'I'm off the hook!'

Dad and Kevin laughed. It wasn't a brilliant joke, but Mam was always encouraging to him, so Kevin wanted to be supportive.

'You can tell it at the youth club tonight,' said Mam, pleased with the joke's reception.

'Actually, there's no meeting tonight,' said Kevin.

'Oh, why's that?' asked Dad.

'We're heading off on camp tomorrow, so we'll be seeing each other morning, noon, and night. Mr Cox said we'd take the night off, and people can pack.'

'Sure I have your stuff already packed,' said his mother.

'Yes, but not everyone's like you, Mam.'

Mam looked pleased at the compliment, but the idea of leaving home left Kevin feeling a little uneasy. The fact that his parents were loving and protective was normally comforting. But next week Kevin couldn't rely on their presence, and he knew that Dennis O'Sullivan had it in for him. It was the one cloud hanging over the holiday, and it had taken some of the good out of the trip to Galway.

On the other hand he was braver now than he used to be. He had, after all, got up the nerve to deflate Vogts' tyre on the day that

Dad had played golf with the two Nazis. It had been a small gesture of defiance, but Kevin had still felt good about striking back, however minor the blow. He remembered how Dad had looked at him in the car park when Vogts had discovered the flat tyre. Nothing had been said, and Vogts had assumed it to be simply a puncture, but Kevin had wondered if perhaps Dad had suspected him of deflating the tyre.

At any rate the combination of his gesture of resistance and his presence at the successful raid at Liffey Junction had stiffened his resolve, and he decided now that he would deal with Dennis O'Sullivan when he had to.

'It's good of Mr Cox to give up a week of his holidays to go away with the youth club,' said Mam as she finished her fish.

'Yes, he's a decent sort,' said Dad. 'I put in a word with Heinrich Vogts, to make sure the group travel permit went smoothly for Mr Cox.'

'I didn't know that,' said Kevin.

Dad smiled. 'There are some perks to being a councillor.'

Kevin felt his hackles rising. 'Some people say we shouldn't need Nazi permission to travel in our own country, Dad.'

His father's smile faded. 'People say a lot of things, Kevin. But the occupation is a fact. Responsible people accept that and get on with it.'

'Responsible people?'

'Yes. Councillors like me, civil servants, tax officials, police officers. They deal with reality, and they must follow German policy.'

'But must they, really, Dad? Can they not at least…be a bit reluctant, a bit slow to do the Nazis' bidding?'

Kevin could see that his mother was uncomfortable with this line of conversation, whereas his father put down his knife and fork and looked annoyed.

'And what would you have them do, Kevin?' he asked. 'Drag their feet when the Nazis issue orders? Where do you think that would leave them?'

'I'm not saying it would be easy. But maybe they don't have to jump to it every time a German gives an order.'

'Defy the Nazis, and *at best* you're out of a job – with no pension, no dole, no way to provide for your family. *At worst* you'll be in a concentration camp or before a firing squad.'

'I didn't say *defy* them, Dad.'

'So what do you suggest? Don't openly defy them, just be sulky and uncooperative?'

'Tom…' said Mam

'No, this needs to be addressed, Una.' Kevin's father looked him in the eye. 'I wish Ireland wasn't occupied. But I don't have the luxury of being snooty to Major Weber. The money I earn paid for your summer camp, money that came in part for working under German orders. Do you want me to cancel your summer camp, so you won't feel tainted?'

'Tom…that's not fair,' said Mam in a rare display of disunity.

Kevin was taken aback by his father's stance and wasn't sure what to say. Before he could figure out a response, Dad breathed out deeply, then raised his hands in a gesture of peace.

'All right. Maybe it *is* unfair to land that choice on a boy.' He turned to Kevin. 'Of course you'll go to summer camp with your friends. But try not to rush to judgement, son. Lots of people are in tricky situations, and they're muddling through as best they can. All right?'

Kevin felt slightly guilty now and he answered quietly. 'All right, Dad.'

'Good lad. Now let's finish our dinner and no more talk of Weber or Vogts or any of them. OK?'

Glad that peace had been restored in the family, Kevin nodded. 'OK, Dad,' he said. 'OK.'

CHAPTER NINETEEN

Roisin threw her suitcase onto the rack above her head, then flopped down on the carriage seat beside Mary. Kevin sat opposite them, and the rest of the train carriage filled up with noisy youth club members whose excitement was mounting as they prepared to set out on the long trip westwards.

They were in Kingsbridge Station, from where the train would bring them to Galway city. In Galway they would transfer to a coach that would take them through the wilds of Connemara to their final destination outside Clifden.

'Settle down, everyone,' said Mr Cox good-humouredly. 'You've a whole week to let your hair down, you don't have to go wild in the first ten minutes!'

There was a slight toning down of the boisterous mood, and Roisin allowed the chatter and the laughter to flow over her. Kevin and Mary were talking animatedly, and for a moment Roisin let her mind wander. She could see Dennis O'Sullivan with his cronies Terry Lawless and Peadar Feeney a little further down the carriage. *What would they think if they knew Dennis was an informer?*

Not that she would tell them. Apart from Aunt Nuala, and Mary and Kevin, she hadn't revealed the secret to anybody. And seeing as she hadn't been taken in for questioning herself, it seemed that Dennis had kept his part of the bargain and had said nothing about her. But the fact that he was a collaborator added tension to an already strained relationship, and Roisin, Kevin and Mary had resolved to be extra careful whenever Dennis was around.

She looked at her friends now and thought how lucky she was to have such good pals. It would be the first holiday any of them had taken without parents or guardians, and Kevin and Mary had both admitted to being slightly nervous as well as excited. Roisin knew that she too would miss Aunt Nuala, who was catching a later train to Mayo, to take her own holidays while Roisin was at camp.

Looking down the carriage, Roisin's gaze fell on Dennis. Just then he looked up. Holding her gaze, he smirked and winked at her. Roisin immediately looked away, irritated by his attitude, and she sensed that things between them were far from settled. Well, she would deal with that when she had to, she decided. Putting Dennis out of her head, she heard a whistle blow. There was a final flurry of activity on the platform, then with a mild jolt the train started forward.

All the youth club members cheered, and Roisin smiled at Kevin and Mary.

'On our way at last,' said Kevin excitedly.

'On our way,' agreed Roisin. 'Here's to a great week.'

The August sunshine flooded in through the carriage window, and

Dennis felt its warmth upon his shoulders. 'The Yanks are such hypocrites!' he said. 'This stuff about America fighting for freedom, it's for the birds.'

'How do you mean?' asked Terry Lawless.

'Exactly what I said,' answered Dennis assuredly.

Their steam train was stopped in Athlone to take on coal and water, and Dennis was enjoying the attention of several boys who sat around him in the carriage listening to his views. Using some of the cash provided by *Kriminalkommissar* Vogts, Dennis had bought sweets for the journey, and his popularity had risen when he had shared his treats with those around him.

'The Americans aren't out for freedom, lads,' said Dennis. 'They're out for themselves, like everybody else. If they really believed everyone should be equal and free, they'd have that in their own country.'

'But isn't America called "The Land of the Free"?' asked Terry.

'That's what they *call* it,' said Dennis. 'That's not what it *is*. The Yanks talk about how the Nazis treat the Jews, but look how *they* treat their own people. Americans who are black have to sit on different park benches, can't eat in white restaurants, even have to use separate toilets.'

Dennis had memorised all this from a newspaper article, but he was careful not to let it sound like he was parroting someone else's views. He could see that the other boys were taken by what he was saying, and he was gratified. At the same time he had to be careful. It was one thing claiming each country was out for its own gain –

as each person should be if he was smart – but he didn't want to appear too pro-Nazi.

'All I'm saying, lads, is that the Germans, the English, the Russians, the French – they do what's best for themselves. So forget the goody-goody talk from the Allies. Sure the Americans didn't even enter the war till they were attacked at Pearl Harbour.'

Dennis saw some of the boys nodding, and he was pleased that his arguments had swayed them. He thought it was important to establish that things weren't black and white, and that there were no obvious good guys. That way if word got out that he had been working for the Germans it needn't be such a big deal.

Not that he was unduly worried. His threat to Roisin Tierney had clearly worked, and she hadn't revealed that he was reporting to *Kriminalkommissar* Vogts. Thinking about Vogts, Dennis was relieved to be having a break from the *Gestapo* man. Vogts paid like clockwork, but Dennis still found him a bit intimidating. In fairness, though, the German had agreed that Dennis could skip his Sunday night report tomorrow, and would instead resume when the week's holiday in Connemara was over. Meanwhile, things weren't standing still. Dennis had been really annoyed with Roisin Tierney and had decided to give her name to Vogts at their last meeting. He had told the German that he had heard she and her aunt might be anti-Nazi. Nothing definite, but a discreet checking of the files might be worthwhile. Dennis had reckoned that if everything was in order then there was no harm done. Whereas if anything showed up, he would have something concrete to use against her. He looked forward to getting an answer – either way – when he returned to Dublin.

For now, though, he would savour his well-earned break, and he dismissed Roisin Tierney from his thoughts and reached into his haversack. He took out a bag of chocolate toffees, and looked at the other boys. 'All right, lads,' he said playfully, knowing this move would cement his popularity. 'Is there anyone here who could tackle a chocolate sweet?!'

Mary watched the sun setting on Clifden Bay, its last rays bathing the scene in a golden glow. The youth club members had reached the campsite late that afternoon and pitched their tents in the grounds of Westwind Estate. The estate had a large manor house that took guests, and a small shop that sold basic groceries and home-made soft drinks to the campers that flocked there in the summer. The site had spectacular views over the Atlantic Ocean that shimmered now in the light of the dipping, red sun. Mary was pleased to be sharing a tent with Roisin, but for the moment she wanted to be alone with her thoughts.

She had headed down the sloping fields towards the sea and sat on an outcrop of rock, eager to open the letter that Mr Cox had delivered to her tent. The youth club leader had joked that Mary must be the apple of someone's eye, to receive a letter that would have been posted before she had even left home. Mary had simply smiled, recognising her father's handwriting, and knowing that the letter *had* indeed been posted before she left home.

She read through it again now, admiring the clever way Dad had written it so that it sounded like he was a friend rather than her father. The letter had been sealed, but on the off-chance of it being read by someone other than Mary, he had phrased everything ambiguously and kept it short.

The essence of the message, however, was that his departure had been brought forward, and he would be leaving tomorrow night. He had suggested seeing Mary one last time at six o'clock tomorrow at the ruins of Clifden Castle.

Mary lowered the letter and tried to come to terms with her feelings. On the one hand she was looking forward to the holiday with her friends, and she was pleased to have the chance to say a last goodbye to Dad. But there was no knowing when she would see him again. And she would miss him badly, though she tried to console herself that when he was in Iceland he would be in less danger than when working with the Resistance in Ireland.

The reality though was that matters were out of her hands, and she just had to make the best of it. So she would try to enjoy the camp, and she would make certain that Dennis O'Sullivan didn't cross paths with Dad tomorrow. After that she would take things a day at a time. Satisfied to have reached some sort of decision, she slipped the letter into her pocket, slid down off the outcrop of rock, and walked back through the warm summer dusk.

PART THREE

AUGUST 1943

SHOWDOWN

'elephone call for you, Kevin,' said Mr Cox. 'It's your father.'

Kevin felt anxious as he crossed the room to take the phone from the youth club leader. He had been with some other boys in the shop at the back of the manor house, and Mr Cox had allowed them to choose from the limited selection of sweets and soft drinks after an afternoon of hiking and swimming.

Kevin and Roisin had resolved to keep a close eye on Dennis O'Sullivan when Mary slipped off to the secret rendezvous with her father, but for now Kevin had been feeling happy and relaxed. A telephone call just one day after he had left home was unexpected, however, and Kevin nervously entered the telephone booth and closed the door after him for privacy. Taking a deep breath, he lifted the phone. 'Dad?'

'Thank God I got you,' said his father.

Kevin knew immediately that something was seriously amiss. 'What's wrong, Dad?'

'Is there anyone within hearing, son?'

'No, I'm in a telephone booth.'

'Even so, keep your voice down, and turn away so no one can see your face.'

'You're scaring me,' answered Kevin, keeping his voice low, as instructed. 'What's happened?'

'Roisin Tierney and her aunt are in danger. Heinrich Vogts led a *Gestapo* raid on Shandon Park, looking for Mrs Tierney.'

'Oh my God!' Kevin gripped the telephone tightly. If Dennis O'Sullivan had decided to get Roisin into trouble, then the *Gestapo* would have come to question her – which would be bad enough. But Dad had said they came for her aunt, Mrs Tierney. Which suggested they had uncovered her role in creating the false identity to hide Roisin's Jewish background.

'Did they say, Dad, what they wanted with Mrs Tierney?'

'I wasn't here when it happened. But Mr Hannigan overheard one of the policemen who was with the Germans. He said they were coming for the Jew.'

Kevin felt his stomach tighten in fear, but he tried not to panic. 'Right,' he said.

'If either of them is Jewish, Kevin, they can't come back to Dublin. You've got to warn Roisin. And she's got to warn her aunt.'

Kevin could barely believe that things had unravelled so quickly. But even as he feared for Roisin and her aunt Nuala, he realised that his own father was taking a risk. Telephone lines weren't secure, and if it ever emerged that he was helping Jews to escape, Dad's life would be in danger, despite his standing as a councillor.

'Make certain you're not seen to be part of any of this, Kevin. That's absolutely vital. But on the quiet, you have to warn Roisin.'

'I'll do it the minute I leave here. But I'll make sure no one sees me.'

'Good lad.'

'And Dad?

'Yes?'

'Thanks for the warning. I know…I know I've been giving you a hard time about the Germans, and I'm sorry now, Dad, I really am.'

'Don't worry about any of that, son.'

'It's still brave what you've done.'

'I can't stand by and see my neighbours murdered. But time is tight here, Kevin. You need to pass on the message as quickly as possible, and like I say, make certain you're not seen doing it. Then if you're asked afterwards, deny all knowledge of any Jewish link.'

'I will. And…and I love you, Dad.'

'I love you too, son. Take care, and God bless.'

'You too.'

Kevin hung up, then stood immobile in the booth as he quickly gathered his thoughts. Somehow, Roisin would have to vanish. And Dennis O'Sullivan had to be kept in the dark. He didn't know how either could be achieved, but he had to find a way. Making an effort to keep his expression untroubled, he stepped out of the booth, left the shop and started back towards the campsite.

* * *

Heavy clouds had come scudding in from the Atlantic, giving

the sea a steely, grey look, but Roisin barely noticed the change from the earlier sunshine. She felt almost paralysed with fear, and recalled that this was how she had felt in her nightmares. But this wasn't a bad dream, this time she had to face the reality of suddenly being unmasked as Jewish.

A few minutes previously Kevin had come to her tent where she had been relaxing with Mary. Kevin had said they needed to talk urgently, and that they had to go somewhere out of sight, but without being seen by Dennis O'Sullivan. Skirting the rest of the tents in the campsite, they had made their way into the thick woods behind the manor house, where Kevin had dropped his bombshell about the *Gestapo* raid on her home. Standing now in the midst of the sweet-smelling woodland, she tried to master her fear and put her thoughts in order.

'I need to get word to Aunt Nuala in Mayo,' she said.

'First you have to escape yourself,' said Kevin.

'No! The first thing is to warn Nuala – I got her into this!'

'You need to do both,' said Mary. 'But let's not panic. There's probably more time than you think.'

'How do you make that out?' asked Kevin.

'It'll take Vogts a good while to get to Clifden. We know how slow the Dublin to Galway train is.'

'They probably have *Gestapo* officers in Galway city,' said Kevin. 'He could send them.'

'Maybe,' answered Mary. 'But it's still a long way out to here.'

'Or he could tell the local police,' said Roisin.

Mary shook her head. 'I doubt he'd trust the local police. Lots of Irish policemen hate working with the Nazis. There's every chance they'd drag their heels.'

'You really think so?'

'Yes,' answered Mary. 'I'm not suggesting we waste a minute of time, but let's not make mistakes by panicking.'

Roisin was reassured by her friend's cool demeanour, and she guessed that Mary must have developed her coolness through involvement with the Resistance. 'You're right,' said Roisin, 'but the first thing is still to get a warning to Aunt Nuala.'

'How do you plan to do that?' asked Kevin.

'There are always a couple of bicycles at the back of the manor house. Supposing I took one and cycled into Clifden? I could send a telegram warning Nuala, then set off and cycle to Mayo myself. It will be dark in a few hours. I could travel by night.'

'What will you say in the telegram?' asked Mary.

'I'll have to find a way to warn her, but in a kind of code.'

'That might make them suspicious in the post office,' said Kevin.

'I'll have to chance that,' said Roisin.

Mary nodded. 'Most people in Connemara are really anti-Nazi. They'll probably turn a blind eye.'

'Fair enough,' said Kevin. 'But as for getting to Mayo, that's a very long cycle.'

'And there's another thing to consider,' suggested Mary.

'What's that?'

'It would be easier for your aunt to disappear, Roisin, if she's only got to worry about herself. If there are two people together, and the Nazis are looking for them as a couple, it will be harder to vanish, even in the wilds of Mayo.'

Roisin hated the idea of being separated from her aunt and she looked at Mary questioningly. 'So what am I supposed to do?'

'I've been thinking about that.'

'And?'

'I've got an idea, but…you probably won't like it.'

'What is it?'

'Just hear me out with an open mind.'

Roisin was impatient to hear Mary's idea and she nodded quickly. 'OK. So, what's your plan?'

Dennis felt on edge. He was standing in the phone booth at the manor house, to which he had been summoned urgently, and he had nervously started to pose a question.

'Listen carefully and don't interrupt me!' said Vogts, his voice sounding crackly down the telephone line.

'Sorry, *Kommissar*,' said Dennis, pressing the telephone to his ear so as not to miss a syllable. He had never heard Vogts so agitated before and he knew that it was essential not to do anything that might upset the German.

'You need to locate Roisin Tierney immediately, then don't let her out of your sight.'

'Yes, *Kommissar.*'

'Though her name *isn't* Roisin Tierney,' continued Vogts. 'She's a Jewess, whose real name is Rachel Clarke.'

Dennis said nothing, stunned by the revelation. His suggestion to check the files had revealed something far more dramatic than he had expected, and he found his head reeling. He had never liked Roisin Tierney – or Rachel Clarke as she apparently was. That wasn't the same as wanting her dead, though, and the exposure of her Jewish background could well be a death sentence. Before he could think about it further, Vogts spoke again. 'I'm just about to leave Dublin by train. Keep a close watch on her until I get to Clifden tonight.'

Dennis realised that this would take hours. A huge responsibility was being placed on him, and he dreaded to think how Vogts would react if anything went wrong. *He had to get out of this.*

'I'm happy to help, of course, *Kommissar*,' he said, 'but would it not speed things up to send officers from Galway?'

'This case is being run from headquarters, I don't want to involve Galway.'

'But the local Garda station in Clifden, could they not hold her till you get here?'

'Don't argue with me! This brat led me a merry dance in Cork. I'm going to arrest her personally. Your job is to watch her till I get there. Is that clear?'

'Yes, *Kommissar.*'

'Do this well and you'll be rewarded. Richly rewarded.'

'Thank you, *Kommissar*.'

'But do not, I repeat, do *not* let her out of your sight. I'm holding you responsible. Don't let me down.'

'No, *Kommissar*.'

'That's all. Go back and locate her, and I'll see you later.'

The German hung up abruptly, and Dennis stood unmoving, then replaced the telephone on its receiver. So Roisin Tierney was really Rachel Clarke. Pretending to be a Catholic while actually Jewish. *What a little liar!* And now she was causing him more trouble, with Dennis being held responsible if she evaded Vogts again. *He couldn't let that happen.*

He had never fully understood why the Nazis were so opposed to the Jews, but the reality was that they were, and he couldn't change that. And if it was a choice between his wellbeing and hers, that was no choice at all. *She had to be arrested.*

He didn't know how she had escaped Vogts in Cork, but he had to make certain she didn't evade the *Gestapo* man a second time. Stepping out of the phone booth, Dennis walked quickly towards the campsite, anxious to find the fugitive he still thought of as Roisin Tierney.

'I need to ask you a huge favour, Dad,' said Mary.

'Oh? What's that?'

Mary paused, trying to find the right words. She had surreptitiously joined her father that afternoon for their farewell meeting in the gloomy ruins of Clifden Castle, but instead of savouring their last moments together she was preoccupied now with how much depended on Dad's answer.

'Spit it out, love,' he said.

'When you go to Iceland tonight, will you bring Roisin with you?'

'What?!'

'The thing is, Dad, she's not really Roisin Tierney. Her real name is Rachel Clarke, and her mother is Jewish. Mrs Tierney doctored the records, but the Germans have found out, and they raided Shandon Park this morning.'

Her father was normally unflappable, but Mary could see that he was shocked.

'When did all this come out?' he asked.

'Just today. Kevin got a phone call from his father, warning him the *Gestapo* had called to Tierneys.'

'Did you know all along she was Jewish?'

'I've known for a while. Though she's *not* actually Jewish, it's her mother who is.'

'That's enough for the Nazis.'

'I know. That's why she has to get away. So I thought if you're leaving the country tonight, she could escape with you.'

'It's not that simple, Mary. She's a lovely girl, and I really sympathise, but I have to see the bigger picture.'

'What does that mean?'

'They sent a submarine because the plans I'm carrying are vital. I can't risk everything by taking Roisin, and bringing the *Gestapo* down on top of me.'

'She's my best friend, Dad. They could murder her!'

Her father said nothing, and Mary looked him in the eye.

'One person boarding the submarine, or two, what's the difference?'

'It's not the submarine, Mary. It's the increased risk of capture with the Germans on her heels.'

'But they wouldn't be on her heels if she's already hiding with you at the meeting point. They'll never expect her to escape by submarine; they won't be looking for that.'

'It still increases the risk. My mission is vital, Mary. It could help change the course of the war.'

'I understand.' Mary took a breath, then looked appealingly to her father. 'So I hate asking you – but I still am. Save my friend's life, Dad. Please?'

CHAPTER TWENTY-ONE

Kevin lay flat on his back. The sweet smell of grass mingled with the odour of canvas as he stretched on the ground sheet inside his tent. Because there was an uneven number of boys on the trip, he had opted for a two-man tent to himself, and now he was glad that he had, as he tried to think things through. His mind was jumbled, but sometimes when he needed to clear his head he found it useful to lie still and try to compose his thoughts. Roisin had gone to Clifden to send her aunt the coded telegram, while Mary had gone for her secret rendezvous with her father, and Kevin knew that he should use this precious time to weigh things up.

No matter how optimistic he tried to be, however, there was no denying that the clock was ticking. It would take Vogts time to travel across the country from Dublin, but if he ordered *Gestapo* officers from Galway to arrest Roisin they could be here much sooner. There was also the risk of the local police turning up. Kevin clung, however, to the fact that the *Gestapo* didn't trust Irish police officers, many of whom they suspected of being anti-Nazi.

If Roisin went to ground with her aunt in the wilds of Mayo a lot would depend on the attitude of the police in the region. Although the Nazis occupied the country, their main bases were in the cities and the towns. German troops were thin on the ground in the more remote areas, so it would mainly be the police that would be on the lookout for the fugitives. That was assuming, of course, that Roisin could get safely from Clifden to Mayo without the authorities intercepting her. On balance, Kevin felt that Mary's plan of escaping by submarine was a better bet, even though it would be tough on Roisin to have to flee to a strange country, and leave behind everyone she knew.

Still, Roisin's first priority had to be staying alive, and Kevin felt that he should persuade his friend to escape to Iceland – assuming that Commandant Flanagan would take her. Kevin hoped that Mary could sell the idea to her father, but there was nothing he could do about that.

Meanwhile the dark, cloudy sky would bring an earlier dusk, which meant there were only a few more daylight hours before the submarine arrived. The priority during that time had to be keeping Dennis O'Sullivan out of the picture.

The more Kevin thought about Dennis, the more he despised him for being an informer. But despising him wasn't enough. He had to be outwitted, and Kevin felt a surge of resolve now. *Whatever it took, he wouldn't let Dennis prevent Roisin's escape.* Dad had taken a risk in sending the warning for Roisin. *Well, he too would take whatever risks were necessary.* And in a battle of wits the first thing a good general did was to find out the location of the enemy, so he would do the same. Rising from the ground, he opened the flap of the tent, stepped outside, and went looking for Dennis O'Sullivan.

* * *

Roisin was on high alert, but she tried to look like she hadn't a care in the world as she cycled into the outskirts of Clifden. She recalled from when she had originally escaped the Nazis and made her way to Dublin that attitude was all-important. *Don't look nervous, don't hesitate, act like what you're doing is perfectly legal and normal.* That way the vast majority of people assume that what you're doing *is* legal and normal.

So far her plan had worked, and she had taken a bicycle from the rear of the manor house without being seen. She had felt slightly guilty about taking something that didn't belong to her. But even as she entertained the thought, she knew that evading the *Gestapo* didn't allow for fine scruples of conscience.

Roisin cycled through the town at a moderate pace that wouldn't draw attention, then slowed to a halt as she approached the main street. She dismounted and propped the bike against the corner of a laneway, deciding to proceed from there on foot. The chances of anyone recognising the bike as being from Westwind House were slim, but it still made sense to be as discreet as possible.

She walked along the main street, the shopfronts looking a little drab under the leaden sky, then she crossed the roadway to the general grocer's that had a sign indicating that it also housed the post office. Her pulses starting to race, Roisin stepped inside and was relieved to find that there were no other customers about. The shop had rows of shelving, and stocked items ranging from tin buckets and Wellington boots to headache powders and thick woollen socks, alongside the milk, bread, and vegetables that would be stocked in any normal grocers.

A stout, middle-aged woman with tight grey curls sat behind the counter. She looked up enquiringly from the Sunday newspaper that she was reading. 'Hello there. What can I get you?' she asked.

Her manner seemed pleasant, and Roisin tried to keep her own tone friendly and relaxed.

'Hello. I'm hoping you can help me. I need to get a telegram to Mayo as soon as I can. I know it's Sunday evening, but it's urgent.'

'I see.'

Please God, thought Roisin, *let her not say it can't be delivered tonight.*

The woman rose from her stool, moved down the counter and returned with a paper form.

Roisin felt her hopes rising, *Then again, the woman hadn't said when it could be delivered.*

'You need to write down the address of the person it's for, and the message,' said the postmistress.

'Grand. And eh…how soon will she get it?' Roisin looked the woman in the eye and tried to make her voice appealing, but without sounding like she was pleading.

'Tonight, if you like. I can send it priority for an extra six pence,' said the woman.

Roisin wanted to cheer, but instead she smiled. 'Thank you,

that's grand.' She wrote down the address of the farm where Nuala was staying with relations, then copied out the message that she had composed in her head while cycling to Clifden. It had taken a while to find phrases that would warn Nuala, yet not sound obviously suspicious. She finished writing the words and handed the form back to the postmistress. Roisin felt her pulses racing as the woman read the message, then looked up.

'Let me read it back to you,' said the post mistress, a hint of query in her voice. '*RACHEL IN SUDDEN DEMAND.* Stop. *SHANDON DAYS FINISHED.* Stop. *JOIN YOU WHEN POSSIBLE.*

'That's it, yes,' said Roisin, trying to sound as if it were a perfectly run-of-the-mill message. She knew that the Rachel reference would alert Nuala that the Germans had discovered her true identity, and that the reference to Shandon Park meant they couldn't return to Dublin. But what did the postmistress make of it all? For a moment the woman held Roisin's gaze, then she nodded.

'That will cost you eight pence for the telegram and sixpence for priority. One and two in total,' she said.

'Fine,' said Roisin, once more hiding her relief. She had brought five shillings of saved pocket money for the week in Connemara, and now she gave the postmistress a two-shilling coin and accepted the change.

Roisin paused. Valuable time was passing, and she knew that the sooner she made her escape the better. But the more she covered her tracks the greater her chances of success when the Germans began asking questions. She tried to calculate how much she could trust the postmistress. She seemed friendly, and helpful, and not too nosey. And hanging on the wall behind her were two small flags, one the maroon and white of Galway's county colours, and the other an Irish tricolour. That suggested to Roisin someone of a nationalist frame of mind who wouldn't be pro-German. Then again, the woman could be a collaborator who left the flags in view to disguise her Nazi sympathies.

Roisin hesitated. Then she took a deep breath and decided to go with her gut instinct. 'I wonder…I wonder if there has to be a record kept of this telegram?' she said.

The postmistress said nothing but looked Roisin squarely in the eye. Roisin could feel her stomach fluttering as the woman opened her mouth to speak.

'All telegrams are recorded,' she said. 'It's the law.'

Roisin tried to hide her disappointment. 'Right.'

'More than my job is worth to be seen breaking the rules.'

'It's just—'

The woman raised a hand, cutting Roisin off. 'What you don't tell me, love I don't know. And what I was going to say was that rules are rules – but records can get lost, or misplaced or forgotten. Sure my memory has gone to the dogs. Chances are I'll have forgotten all about you the minute you leave the shop.'

Roisin could hardly believe her luck. 'Thank you so much,' she said.

'I don't know your situation, love,' said the woman. 'But these are hard times, so I wish you well. Go carefully.'

'I will. And thank you again.'

'God bless.'

'God bless.' Roisin nodded then turned away, her spirits lifted as she stepped out the door.

Dennis kicked a nettle in frustration as he strode though the field in which the youth club members were camping. Roisin Tierney wasn't in her tent. She hadn't been at the shop at the manor house, and she was nowhere to be seen around the campsite. Vogts would be furious if Dennis let her slip through his fingers, but he put the thought of failure from his mind and tried to think logically. The chances were that Roisin was around somewhere. She could have gone for a walk, or a swim, in which case he would see her sooner or later.

On the other hand, she could have fled already. If Dennis could be alerted by phone it was possible that Roisin had been alerted too. But even if she had, escape would be a challenge. Clifden was a remote spot on the western seaboard whose rail link had been discontinued several years previously. And with petrol strictly rationed, getting about by road transport was difficult. No, the chances were that she was still in the vicinity. He needed to hold his nerve, locate her, and then keep her under close watch until

Vogts arrived.

He saw Mr Cox approaching across the field and he made a conscious effort to sound casual as the youth leader drew near.

'Ah, Mr C. You haven't seen Roisin Tierney, have you?'

'No, not for a while. Anything the matter?'

'No. No…just wanted a word.'

'Here's Kevin,' said Mr Cox, pointing. 'He might know where she is.'

The youth club leader moved on, and Dennis found himself face to face with Kevin Burke. Dennis drew himself up to his full height, then stood in the way of the smaller boy. 'Where's Roisin Tierney?' he demanded.

'How would I know?'

Dennis was surprised by the response. Normally Kevin avoided confrontation, but tonight he didn't seem in any way intimidated. *Time to be more aggressive.* 'You'd know, because you're like her little lapdog! Now where is she?'

'I don't know,' said Kevin. 'But if I *did* know, you'd be the last person I'd tell.'

'Really?' said Dennis threateningly.

Kevin didn't retreat, however, but instead spoke calmly. 'We know you're an informer. But just once in your life you should do the right thing.'

Dennis felt his temper rising and he stared Kevin in the eye. 'Really? And what's the right thing?'

'Say nothing. Or if the Germans ask, say Roisin has vanished.'

Despite his anger Dennis was taken aback by the other boy's coolness and the audacity of what he was suggesting. 'And why would I do that?' he asked.

'Because the Nazis could *kill* her. Even you must know that's wrong.'

Dennis felt uncomfortable and he hesitated before replying. 'It's out of my hands what the Nazis do.'

'No, it's not. You could easily sing dumb. You really *ought* to, for your own sake.'

'For my own sake?'

'If Roisin is killed by the Nazis because of you, do you think that'll be the end of it? Do you really think nothing can happen to you?'

'Are you…are you threatening me, Burke?'

Kevin paused, then nodded his head. 'I am actually. We're not playing games anymore. Lives are at stake – including yours. So you need to think again if you believe you're untouchable.'

Dennis hadn't expected to have his life threatened – least of all by Kevin Burke – and for a moment he was dumbfounded.

'Think very carefully about your next move,' said Kevin. 'And do the right thing.'

Before Dennis could respond, the other boy turned on his heel and walked away. Dennis stood immobile, trying to come to terms with what had happened. Kevin's new-found backbone had taken him completely by surprise. And the calm way he had made his threat was actually more unsettling than if he had ranted and raved. Despite the Nazis killing hostages in reprisal, the Resistance sometimes *did* shoot collaborators. But had Kevin Burke got links to the Resistance or was he just bluffing? And even if he meant his threat, was it not equally risky – in fact, more risky – for Dennis to mislead *Kriminalkommissar* Vogts? The Nazis were totally ruthless, and if Vogts discovered that he had played a role in helping Roisin Tierney to escape, he would pay with his life.

Dennis stood in the middle of the field weighing up his options. Then he made up his mind and started back towards his tent.

The heady scent of pine filled the evening air in the thick woods at the northern end of the campsite as Mary and Kevin anxiously awaited Roisin's return. The two friends had taken a roundabout route to make sure that nobody saw them entering the woods, and the overcast sky and heavy tree cover meant that the gloomy interior of the woods was a good hiding place. Kevin had seen no sign of Dennis O'Sullivan, and he had been sketching to pass the time, but now he stopped.

'Listen!' he said.

Mary strained her ears, then heard the sound of someone moving in the distance. Wordlessly she followed Kevin's example and slipped off the trail and deeper into the trees. She heard the sound of a snapping twig, and they both stood stock still. Some-one was drawing nearer along the trail, and Mary swallowed hard, hoping it was her friend.

Suddenly Roisin came into view, and Mary relaxed.

'Roisin! Over here!' she called softly.

Roisin waved and started towards them.

'Thank God,' said Kevin, as she reached them. 'I was starting to get really worried.'

'How did it go?' asked Mary.

'Fine. I borrowed a bike at the manor house and I've just left it back where I found it.'

'And the telegram?' asked Kevin.

'It's being sent. And the postmistress was sound. She'll say nothing.'

'Brilliant!' said Mary.

'And no police activity in Clifden?' queried Kevin.

Roisin shook her head. 'No. Not yet, anyway.' She turned to Mary. 'How did your part go?'

'I met Dad, and we said our goodbyes.' Mary could feel a lump in her throat as she said the words, but she knew she couldn't afford to dwell on her sadness right now. 'The good thing is he'll take you with him. The submarine is coming tonight.'

'Oh Mary. Thank you so much – and your dad. I'll never…I'll never be able to thank you enough,' said Roisin.

Mary could hear the emotion in her friend's voice, and she felt a surge of affection for her. She knew that despite needing to escape, Roisin was frightened by the idea of leaving her family and friends for a country where she knew nobody. She reached out and squeezed Roisin's arm in sympathy. 'Don't worry about thanks. Just get yourself safely on the sub with Dad.'

'What time is it coming?'

'As soon as it gets dark. Dad wants you to meet him at half nine on the shore road. He has a rowing boat hidden nearby.'

'That's nearly three hours away, though. What do I do till then?'

'You've got to lie low,' said Kevin. 'Dennis O'Sullivan was looking for you.'

'Oh, God,' said Roisin.

'No, it should be fine. He seemed to be acting off his own bat rather than with the police. I told him I'd no idea where you were. And I told him to keep his mouth shut as well. I eh…well, I threatened him that if anything happened to you, he'd pay a huge price. I think maybe it got through to him.'

'Thanks, Kevin. So, we hide out here?' said Roisin.

'Not for the whole time,' answered Kevin.

'When it's time for you to make your move,' suggested Mary, 'we could use a diversion.'

Roisin looked at her. 'Like what?'

'I've been weighing up ideas,' said Mary with a hint of a grin. 'And I think I've got just the thing…'

A light breeze blew in off the sea, giving the air a tang of salt. The low cloud made for a gloomy atmosphere, but dusk proper was still some way off. Kevin looked at his watch again as he crouched hidden in the trees observing the rear of the manor house. It was nearly seven o'clock, which meant that there was still almost two hours to go before Roisin set off for her rendezvous with Commandant Flanagan. Timing was going to be critical, Kevin reckoned, and everything could change if the local police suddenly showed up. But so far there had been no sign of either *Gestapo* officers from Galway or local police from Clifden, and Kevin's instinct was that *Kriminalkommisar* Vogts wanted to arrest Roisin himself. Which meant that Vogts' travel plans were the key consideration.

Kevin went back over his calculations. *The call from Dad, warning him that Vogts was looking for Roisin, had been at about five o'clock. Say Vogts got to a westbound train within half an hour of that - 5.30 p.m. The train driver might have to stop in Athlone to take on water for the steam engine, but Vogts could still be in Galway by 8.00 pm. Say another hour and a half to drive from Galway out to Clifden and then on the campsite — 9.30 pm.*

Kevin bit his lip, wishing they had more leeway. If everything went to plan, Roisin should have enough time to get away. But if anything went wrong, or if Vogts made better time, things could get messy.

Suddenly Kevin's speculation was cut short by a movement from the rear of the manor house. The farm manager, Mr O'Brien, stepped out the door of one of the outhouses. He was a heavyset, middle-aged man and he moved ponderously. He stopped at a tap in the yard and rinsed his hands before going in the back door of the manor house. Kevin's heart began to race. He reasoned that having washed his hands, Mr O'Brien was gone for his tea. It was the chance Kevin had been waiting for, and he rose from his crouching position and walked speedily towards the outhouse.

Earlier in the day Kevin had been drawing cartoons when Mr Cox had asked him to run an errand. It had involved tracking down Mr O'Brien in the outhouse, where the farm manager had given him a container of disinfectant that Mr Cox needed for the latrines used by the campers. The container had been stored in the outhouse, alongside weedkiller, plant sprays and other farming equipment. The item that had caught Kevin's attention, however, had been a double-barrelled shotgun, hung by a strap from a wall rack at the end of the room.

The shotgun was what Kevin had come for now, and as he quietly swung open the door of the outhouse, he prayed that it would still be there. Kevin stepped inside, softly closing the door after him. His heart was thumping, and he knew it would be hard to talk his way out of this if he were caught now. Dismissing the thought, he moved down the room and saw that the gun was still on the rack.

Kevin reached up and took the weapon down. He had never fired a shotgun, but he knew how they worked, and he quickly broke it open to check if it was loaded. To his relief there was a cartridge in each barrel. He paused, aware that there could be no going back from this action. In recent times he had done lots of things that were illegal. This was different though, and he knew he was crossing a boundary. But Roisin's life was at stake tonight, and if *Kriminalkommissar* Vogts arrived to capture her then having a weapon might be crucially important. Without further ado he snapped the gun closed. Then he slung the weapon from his shoulder, turned around and made for the door.

Dennis walked through the campsite, trying not to let his worry show. The other youth club members were relaxing, some playing football, some chatting at their tents, some tending fires on which billy cans were being boiled. Normally Dennis would have enjoyed being at the centre of things. Instead he felt increasingly frustrated by Roisin Tierney's absence.

Without making it too obvious, Dennis had searched the campsite for her, but to no avail.

And then there was the matter of Kevin Burke. The more Dennis thought about it, the more furious he was at the way Kevin had threatened him. He couldn't let him away with that, and as soon as possible he wanted to settle the score. Which wasn't to say that Burke's threat was necessarily an idle one. But if it came to fearing the Resistance, or fearing the Nazis, Dennis knew where the power lay. The Nazis ruled Ireland with an iron fist, and until such time as they were ousted, he would support the winning side.

He had to stay on the right side of Vogts, and find Roisin Tierney before the *Gestapo* man reached Clifden. *Time to move up a gear and get some help*, he thought.

He rounded a large oak tree under which several tents were pitched, then came across Terry Lawless and Peadar Feeney sitting outside their tent. Terry was carving a stick with his scout knife, and Peadar was reading a comic, but they both looked up when Dennis approached.

'I need you to help me with something, lads,' he said.

'What's that?' asked Terry.

'I've been looking for Roisin Tierney but I can't find her. I'll give you a toffee bar each if you help me find her.'

'Why do you want to find Roisin Tierney?' asked Peadar.

'I don't need to be quizzed, Peadar. Do you want the bar or not?'

'I want it!'

'I thought you didn't like Roisin,' said Terry.

'I don't, but I need to talk to her.' Dennis deliberately kept his answers vague, thinking that if she was arrested and taken away he could claim afterwards that he had been trying to tip her off. That way it would be his word against Kevin's when it came to the collaborator accusation. First though Roisin had to be found. 'Well, are you going to sit there, or do you want to help?' he asked.

'We'll help,' answered Terry. He dropped the wood that he was carving, slipped the scout knife into his pocket and rose to his feet.

Peadar rose also, folding his comic and putting it into the back pocket of his trousers. 'And Dennis,' he said a look of concern on his face, 'that's not a toffee bar between us, that's a bar each, right?'

'Yes, Peadar, I *said* a bar each.'

'Grand.'

'OK, then,' said Dennis. 'We need to search every inch of the estate till we find her. Let's go!'

* * *

Roisin gripped her binoculars tightly, horrified by what she was seeing. 'Oh my God,' she said softly.

'What is it?' asked Mary.

They were perched high in the fork of a tree in the woods, camouflaged by evergreen pine branches and by chestnut trees that were heavily in leaf.

'Roisin?' pressed Mary.

'It's Dennis O'Sullivan. He's recruited Terry Lawlesss and Peadar Feeney.'

'Recruited them? For what?'

'To find me, I'd say. He's making hand signals for them to head up this way. It looks like he's going to search down towards the sea.'

'Are they definitely headed towards here?'

Roisin waited a moment, praying that the two boys might veer off in some other direction. Instead she felt her heart sinking as they started towards the woods. 'Yes,' she answered, 'right this way.'

'Why don't I intercept them?' suggested Mary. 'I can send them on a wild goose chase.'

'They won't believe you?'

'Why not?'

'Because we don't like them. So why would you suddenly co-operate? They'd smell a rat.'

'They mightn't, Roisin. They're not the brightest.'

'I know. But even so, I can't see them swallowing it.'

'So what do we do?'

Roisin thought a moment then turned to Mary. 'We stay here. People tend not to look up when they're searching for something. If we stay absolutely still they won't see us.'

Roisin could see that her friend was dubious and she tried to reassure her. 'Look on the bright side. If they search the woods and don't find us, it's a double bonus.'

'How's that?'

'It means I can stay here till it gets dark. They won't come back to the woods if they've already searched there, so I'll be safe.'

Mary looked thoughtful. 'I hadn't looked at it that way.'

'It's our best chance. All we have to do is keep our nerve, and not move a muscle.'

'OK.'

Kevin carefully skirted the manor house, making sure that nobody saw him as he headed towards the avenue leading to the estate entrance. He kept the shotgun held low and carried it as inconspicuously as possible. Nevertheless, if anyone spotted him with the weapon the game would be up. He moved briskly, his stomach tight with tension as he skirted a field of waist-high corn.

He had to hide the gun, and the sooner the better. The challenge was to find someplace from which he could retrieve it quickly if Vogts arrived to capture Roisin. At the same time the hiding place had to be somewhere that nobody would stumble upon in the meantime. And he had to be able to locate the shotgun in the dark.

There was a large hay barn on the opposite side of the avenue, and Kevin had thought of hiding the shotgun under a bale of hay. But what if one of the farm workers was ordered to collect fodder from the barn and discovered the gun? Or if the building was locked at night for fear of thieves stealing the hay?

Kevin stopped, knowing he needed a better idea. And then it hit him. The corn was waist-high, and they wouldn't be harvesting it tonight. Looking about to make certain he was unobserved, Kevin stepped into the field a little further up the avenue. He made sure to pick an entry point in line with a willow tree on the far side of the avenue, so that he would have a landmark. About three feet into the thick stalks of corn he lowered the shotgun to the ground. It would be invisible from the avenue, yet easily retrievable. Satisfied with his choice, Kevin stepped out of the corn and onto the avenue again, his mind racing.

He had never used a gun in his life, and he wondered what would happen if he had to do it now. Could he really shoot another person? And would he be brave enough to exchange fire with the Nazis? Then he thought about Roisin, and what would happen if Vogts captured her, and his resolve stiffened. *He had to make sure she escaped, no matter what.* He hoped that could be done without confronting the Germans, but if not, then so be it. Feeling nervous but determined, he started back for the campsite.

Dennis strode towards the woods, his irritation growing. There was still no sign of Roisin Tierney, despite his having searched every belt of trees, and every clump of bushes along the western boundary of the estate. *Where had she gone?* It was possible that she had already fled. But she wouldn't get far travelling on foot, especially with darkness coming soon, and Dennis reckoned that Roisin Tierney was too smart to do something that had little chance of success. Which meant she was likely to be still somewhere in the vicinity.

He reached the top of the field, just as Terry and Peadar emerged from the woods.

'Ah, Dennis,' said Terry. 'You didn't find here either?'

'No,' answered Dennis, irked by the casual way that Terry was accepting defeat. 'Did you search all the woods?

'Yeah, we had a look,' said Peadar. 'No sign of her.'

'You had a look, or you searched?'

'What's the difference?'

Dennis made a conscious effort to keep his patience. '*Having a look*, is easy-going, Peadar. *Searching*, is making a proper effort.'

'What's the big deal, anyway?' asked Terry.

Dennis hesitated. 'If I tell you this, you have to keep it to your-selves, OK?'

'OK.'

'Peadar?'

'Sure.'

'I heard a whisper,' said Dennis. 'Don't ask me how, just trust me that I heard it.'

'A whisper about what?' asked Terry.

'That Roisin Tierney is in trouble with the Germans. I don't like her much, but I don't want to see her falling into the hands of the *Gestapo*. So we need to find her and tip her off, but without anyone knowing that's what we're doing. OK?'

'OK,' answered Peadar.

'What about us?' asked Terry. 'If the Germans find out we helped her—'

'They won't,' interjected Dennis. 'If she gets away it doesn't come up. And if they catch her, that's all they'll care about. Tip-ping her off won't come into it, they'll already *have* her. Either way we've nothing to worry about. All right?'

'Fair enough,' said Peadar.

'Terry?'

'Yeah, all right.'

'Good. So come on, let's do the woods again. And this time, we don't take a look – we search.'

* * *

'Oh no,' said Mary, the binoculars pressed tightly to her eyes.

'What's wrong?' asked Roisin.

They were still hidden up the tree, relieved that Terry Lawless and Peadar Feeney had departed uneventfully.

'They're coming back!' whispered Mary.

'What?'

'And Dennis is with them.' Mary lowered the binoculars and saw how worried Roisin looked. When Roisin spoke, however, she managed to keep her voice calm. 'We have to do the same as before. Don't stir an inch.'

'I won't. But Dennis is smarter than them; he mightn't be so lackadaisical.'

'All the more reason not to move a muscle.'

Before Mary could respond Roisin raised a finger to her lips for silence. Mary nodded in understanding. The boys had gone from sight now, but after a moment Mary heard them making their way through the trees.

Her mouth had gone dry and she could feel beads of perspiration on her forehead but she resisted the temptation to mop her brow. The slightest movement might catch the eye of one of the boys if he happened to glance up.

The searchers had fanned out a little, and as they drew nearer Mary heard Dennis telling them to slow down, and to check every nook and cranny. She found herself holding her breath as they got closer. *Please, God, don't let them look up,* she prayed. Suddenly she heard a twig snapping right below her, and her heart pounded in her chest. Roisin was sitting stock still beside her, but Mary didn't even glance at her friend, instead holding herself totally immobile and resisting the temptation to look down. This was the moment of truth. If the boy below looked up, she could be seen, despite the heavy summer foliage. Time seemed to freeze, and Mary bit her lip, dreading to hear a cry of discovery. Then the boy began to move off. Slowly and noiselessly she breathed out. Neither girl moved until the sound of the searching boys gradually died away as they moved on through the woods.

'Oh my God, that was nerve-wracking,' said Mary softly.

Roisin nodded. 'My heart was in my mouth.'

'But like you said. Now that they've ruled out the woods, you can stay here till it's time to go.'

'Yeah,' answered Roisin. 'Though I've got a feeling – this could be the longest two hours of my life.'

CHAPTER TWENTY-TWO

The light was fading fast, and Roisin found herself struggling with mixed emotions. On one hand she was relieved that no one had discovered her hiding place in the woods and that she had finally been able to climb down from her perch in the tree. On the other hand, the time was nearly here for her departure, and she couldn't help but feel sad. She knew that by fleeing the country she was giving Aunt Nuala a better chance of disappearing. But she dreaded saying goodbye to Kevin and Mary, with no idea of when she would see them again. If she *ever* saw them again.

Mary claimed that Commandant Flanagan was confident the Allies would win in the end. But supposing they didn't? Supposing the invasion failed, and the Nazis were the ones who won? She might be stuck indefinitely in Iceland, never to see Mam and Dad, or Aunt Nuala, or Mary and Kevin again. *No*, she thought, *she had to stay positive*.

'It's nearly time,' said Kevin, breaking her reverie. He indicated his wristwatch, whose luminous dial could be seen in the gloom.

'OK,' said Roisin.

'I hate these goodbyes,' said Mary with a catch in her voice. 'First Dad, now you.'

'Me too,' said Roisin struggling to keep her own voice from

breaking. She knew that a quick farewell would spare her the sadness that she suspected they were all trying to hide. But tempting as it was to end things quickly, Roisin thought that she owed it to her friends to tell them how she felt. 'I just want to say...' she began haltingly. 'I can't thank you enough for all you're done. You've risked so much and...well, you're the two best friends I've ever had. You're the best friends *anyone* could *ever* have.'

'Thanks, Roisin,' said Kevin. 'You're a brilliant friend too.'

'Yes, thanks, Ro,' said Mary, her voice thick with emotion. 'I'm going to miss you so much.'

Roisin felt the tears welling up in her eyes. 'If I say...if I say any more I'll crack up. Just give me a hug.'

Mary stepped forward and the two girls hugged each other wordlessly. Then Roisin turned to Kevin and hugged him tightly in farewell.

'Take care, Roisin,' he said as he let her go.

'I will.'

'And we'll meet again,' he added, 'and be best friends again when this is over. Let's make that a promise.'

'Absolutely,' said Roisin.'

'That's a promise,' agreed Mary solemnly.

'All right, time to divert everyone's attention,' said Kevin. 'Are you ready?'

'Yes,' answered Roisin, her heart already beginning to pound. 'Let's do it.'

Dennis stepped back from the heat of the blazing barn, its dry timber walls crackling as the bales of hay within it burned furiously. The flames leaped up, silhouetted against the darkening night sky.

'Dennis, join the line!' cried Mr Cox, indicating a line of campers who were passing along buckets of water to help douse the flames

Almost everyone from the campsite had run to watch the spectacle of the burning barn, and Dennis could see that while helping with the buckets, the other club members were nevertheless enjoying the drama of the situation. There was no sign of Roisin Tierney, however, which was worrying. Surely anyone still on the campsite would be drawn to the drama of the blazing barn?

'Come on, Dennis!' cried Mr Cox.

'OK, OK!' answered Dennis, reluctantly joining the line of helpers.

He passed on buckets of water that were filled at the nearest pump, but even as he did so he reckoned it was a waste of time. The fire had taken hold, and it would take more than buckets of water passed laboriously from hand to hand to extinguish it.

Meanwhile, in all this confusion, Roisin Tierney might slip away unnoticed if she had been hiding. She might even have started the fire to keep everyone distracted. Or was he letting his imagination run away with him? No, he thought, she was both in danger and determined, and that was a powerful combination. All the more reasons to redouble his own efforts to find her. Because having to tell a furious Vogts that he had failed him was something Dennis didn't want to think about.

He waited until Mr Cox moved out of sight. Then he passed on one more bucket of water, stepped out of the line of helpers, and moved off, his eyes peeled as he searched for Roisin Tierney.

Mary felt guilty as she watched the blazing barn. She had made her way from the woods to the barn a few minutes previously, then carried out her planned diversion by setting the hay alight. The barn and its contents were the property of the Westwind Estate, and Mary hoped that they would be covered by insurance. But even if they weren't, Roisin's life was at stake here. However bad Mary felt about destroying farm property – and Mam had always taught her to respect other peoples' possessions – it was surely justified, Mary reasoned, if it meant that her friend escaped unobserved from the campsite.

She felt a wave of heat emanating from the blaze, and the smoke stung her eyes, but she kept her place in the human chain that Mr Cox had formed, and made sure to be seen playing her part in passing on the buckets of water.

All around her the other youth club members were gathered, some of them active in the human chain, others mesmerised by the spectacle of the blaze. *Good*, she thought, because just about now Roisin should be making for the avenue that led to the estate entrance, and the road that snaked down to the coast. And if all went well, less than an hour after that Roisin and Dad would be on the submarine. *If all went well…* Praying it would, Mary passed on the buckets of water, while the flames from the burning barn licked up into the night sky.

Kevin heard the ringing of the alarm bell on an approaching vehicle and his stomach fluttered. From where he was standing watching the burning barn he couldn't see if it was a fire brigade or a police car that was drawing nearer. *Please, God, let it be the fire brigade,* he thought. He knew that police cars also used bells when on their way to emergencies, but he tried to convince himself that if Vogts were arriving in a *Gestapo* vehicle he would want to give no warning of his approach

Kevin found himself holding his breath as the sound of the vehicle drew closer. Its lights flashing, and the bell still ringing, a fire tender came around the bend in the avenue and screeched to a halt close to the barn. Kevin breathed out, relieved for the moment. He knew that the danger to Roisin was far from over. Under cover of the confusion of the fire she would have slipped away by now. But she had to rendezvous with Commandant Flanagan, row out in a boat, and board the submarine. It could still end in disaster if Vogts suddenly arrived on the scene.

The firemen were jumping down from their tender now, and with people distracted by all the drama, Kevin chose to make his move. Without telling Roisin, who already had enough to worry about, he had decided to act as her back up. He would collect the hidden shotgun and follow her to the rendezvous point. With luck everything would go to plan and he wouldn't have to do anything. But if Vogts arrived at the crucial moment, Kevin could open fire and perhaps buy Roisin enough time to get away.

Stepping back from the glow of the burning building, he entered the shadows, turned on his heel and walked off into the night.

Dennis stopped dead. He had been searching the area between the burning building and the entrance avenue in a vain attempt to find Roisin. Now he had caught a glimpse of Kevin Burke heading off into the dark. Immediately Dennis was on the alert. The blazing hay barn and the arrival of the fire brigade made for quite a spectacle. Why would Burke turn his back on that? Unless, of course, he had something more pressing to do. Like meeting Roisin Tierney.

Acting on instinct, Dennis set off after the other boy. It would be the perfect payback for Burke's earlier arrogance if he now unwittingly led the way to Roisin's hiding place. It was important, though not to let him know he was being followed, and Dennis stayed well back,

The light from the fire was enough to show Kevin as a barely visible shape in the distance as he made his way up the avenue. Dennis lost sight of him for a moment, then caught a glimpse of the other boy emerging from the edge of the cornfield that bordered the avenue. What was he doing in the cornfield? Collecting something for Roisin? Before Dennis could decide, he lost sight of Kevin again. It was obvious that he was making his way up the avenue towards the entrance to the estate. Dennis kept his distance, then was rewarded with a fleeting glimpse of his quarry when Kevin swiftly passed the lighted window of the gatekeeper's cottage.

The light from the cottage window cast a small pool onto the roadway at the right-hand side of the gate. Kevin never stepped through it, however, which meant that he must have turned left. Dennis paused a moment, thinking things through. The right turn led east, back towards Clifden. But the left turn led westwards, with the road winding down towards the shoreline of Clifden Bay.

Was that where Roisin was hiding? Maybe she was planning to get away in a rowing boat. Maybe she had even bribed a fisherman to help her escape in a trawler. Then again, Kevin's slipping away might have nothing to do with Roisin. Supposing he had just met some local girl and they had made a date? There was no way of knowing for sure, but Dennis's gut feeling was that Kevin's sudden disappearance had to do with Roisin Tierney. *He would follow the other boy and see where it led.* Taking care not to make a sound, Dennis moved off after his quarry.

Roisin looked up in alarm as the rising moon peeped through a break in the clouds. Normally she loved the soft glow of moonlight, but tonight darkness had been her friend. She stopped on the narrow road that led down to the sea, hoping the earlier thick cloud cover would return. Not far ahead she could make out where the road joined the shoreline; then as suddenly as it had appeared, the moon vanished behind a bank of cloud.

Roisin continued, knowing that she was nearing the rendezvous point. She had encountered no traffic on the road so far, but she still moved cautiously taking care to make as little noise as possible. She heard the sound of lightly lapping waves, then realised that she was almost at the waterline. This was where she was to meet Commandant Flanagan. But on reaching the spot she couldn't see anyone.

She felt her anxiety mounting. Having got this far, it would be unbearable if something went wrong and the submarine didn't show up. Or if Commandant Flanagan couldn't make it, or worse, if he had already been captured by the Germans. Just then she heard a sudden movement to her right and she started badly.

'Roisin, over here!' whispered a man's voice.

She immediately recognised it as the voice of her friend's father,

and she felt a surge of relief. 'Thank God,' said Roisin. 'I was praying you'd be here.'

She moved across the roadway and found herself face to face
with Commandant Flanagan.

'No problems getting away?' he asked anxiously.

'No.'

'And no one followed you, or saw you leaving?'

'No, they were distracted by a fire that Mary started. Everything
went to plan.'

'Good.'

'And thank you so much for taking me.'

'You're grand, 'said Commandant Flanagan dismissively. 'But
you need to wait here while I get the rowing boat. It will just take
a few minutes.'

'Fine.'

'First, though, I need to send a signal.'

Roisin realised that he was carrying a torch, which he pointed
out towards the sea, flashing the light several times in a regular
sequence. Roisin couldn't see any vessels in the darkness and she
turned to Commandant Flanagan. 'Is the submarine already here?'

'It hasn't surfaced yet. But its periscope should be up watching
for my signal.'

'How can you be sure they saw it?'

'We can't be sure. But the location is right, the time is right, and
the signal is right. So we do what we always do.'

'What's that?'

'Be ready for the worst, but hope for the best.'

'OK, then,' said Roisin. 'Let's hope for the best.'

Kevin saw the flashing light in the distance and he slipped the shotgun off his shoulder, coming to an immediate stop at the side of the road. He paused, waiting to see if the signal would be flashed out again. And it *was* a signal, he felt sure, with its sequence too regular to be anything but a message. Surely it had to be Commandant Flanagan making contact with the submarine. Unless the Resistance had been betrayed, in which case it could be the Nazis, flashing the light to lure the submarine into a trap.

But assuming it *was* Commandant Flanagan, and everything was going as planned, it was still much too soon to relax. Vogts could arrive at any moment, and until Roisin and Commandant Flanagan were safely below the waves Kevin had to be on guard.

The signal wasn't repeated, and after a moment Kevin looked behind him. All he could see was darkness with the blazing barn well out of sight. Good, he thought. It meant that if Germans arrived by road he would see their headlights and have advance warning of their approach. Because whatever it took, he had to make sure that Roisin and Commandant Flanagan got to Iceland.

He didn't want to spook Roisin by drawing attention to the fact that she was in danger up to the moment she boarded the submarine. Instead he would get closer, check discreetly that it wasn't the Germans who had flashed the light, and then continue in his role of unseen back up. Hoisting the shotgun back up onto his shoulder, he started off again down the darkened road.

Dennis stood unmoving as he gathered his thoughts. He had seen the light flashing and reckoned that something illegal was going on, but he tried not to jump to conclusions.

It might have nothing to do with Roisin; it could be smugglers, or gun-runners or something else illicit. Then again it could be a signal for Roisin to rendezvous with Kevin Burke. Before he could ponder it further, the clouds parted again and a bright yellow half moon broke through. Dennis punched the air in triumph. For there, in the distance, silhouetted against the sea in the moonlight, was Roisin Tierney, standing at the water's edge.

As had been the case before, the period of moonlight was brief, and the clouds soon blocked the light once more. Dennis still felt elated, however. *He had found his target.* Clearly Kevin *was* meeting Roisin, and Dennis savoured the irony that after all his bravado, Kevin had unwittingly revealed her hiding place.

So what was their plan? Meeting by the shoreline was hardly a chance decision; it suggested a probable escape by water. Had Kevin obtained a rowing boat for her? Or maybe arranged for a local trawlerman to spirit her away?

Not that it mattered. Dennis knew exactly where she was, and it was up to him to stop her escaping. It looked like Vogts would be too late in arriving now. But if Dennis apprehended Roisin – and gave Kevin an enjoyable beating in the process – then Vogts would be hugely in his debt. Eager to bring matters to a head, Dennis started down the road again.

Roisin sat down distractedly on a rock at the waterline, her emotions in turmoil. She was truly grateful to Commandant Flanagan for agreeing to bring her with him, and to Kevin and Mary for all the risks they had taken on her behalf. She was excited too, now that she was on the brink of escaping by submarine.

And yet. No matter how illogical it was, part of her felt guilty, as though she were abandoning her mother and her aunt. She knew she couldn't help Mam in Spike Island, and that Aunt Nuala should be able to go to ground safely in Mayo, but she still hated the idea of her escaping and their being left behind. And becoming a refugee herself in Iceland, where she knew nobody and didn't speak the language, was a daunting prospect.

No doubt Commandant Flanagan would look after her as best he could, but he would be returning to Ireland as soon as possible. What would she do then? Realistically, she couldn't return home until the Allies invaded successfully and liberated the country, and there was no telling how long that might take.

Could Dad survive in a German work camp till then, or Mam

in the difficult conditions of Spike Island? All she could do was pray they would, and make certain she survived herself. So that's what she would concentrate on, she decided. Other people had risked a lot to save her, so she would strive to live the kind of worthwhile life denied to those who had fallen victims to the Nazis. Steeled in her resolve, she looked out to sea, and waited as patiently as she could for Commandant Flanagan to return.

Kevin heard a sound in the darkness behind him. He had hung back silently a couple of hundred yards from the rocks where he had seen Roisin. Now, though, his heart suddenly pounded. *Someone was approaching along the road*. Kevin acted quickly, hoping to avoid whoever was drawing near. He was standing by a gate set into the field adjoining the road, and he decided to climb the gate to avoid whoever was approaching. He placed his foot on the first bar of the gate and was horrified when it sagged under his weight and made a loud creaking noise. Kevin stopped dead, then looking behind him, saw in the starlight the faint outline of another person.

'That you, Burke? I reckon it must be. Come out and show your face!'

Kevin recognised the voice at once and could hardly believe his ears. *How on earth had Dennis O'Sullivan found them?* He tried to think quickly. However Dennis had done it, he was here now, and the threat he represented had to be contained.

Kevin turned around to face him.

'You thought you were so clever,' said Dennis, his tone mocking as he drew nearer. 'Hiding your little pal away, and then starting a fire to distract everyone. But you weren't so smart in the end, were you? You actually *led* me to her.'

'I don't know what you're talking about.'

'Don't play dumb. I saw her in the distance when the moon came out. The game is up, Burke, *Kommissar* Vogts is on his way. And he's really keen to get his hands on Roisin Tierney.'

Kevin felt a surge of anger but kept his voice calm. 'No one's getting their hands on Roisin Tierney.'

'No? Try to interfere, and I'll punch your lights out. And this time I *will* break your arm.'

'I don't think so,' said Kevin. Then in one swift movement he reached down, grabbed the shotgun from the ground and aimed it at Dennis. 'Both barrels are loaded. Raise your voice, or make a move, and I swear to God, I'll blow your head off!'

Roisin suddenly stiffened. She had been listening for the sound of Commandant Flanagan approaching in the rowing boat. Instead she had heard what sounded like someone's voice in the distance. She looked anxiously in the direction of the road. Nothing was visible in the darkness, however, and despite straining her ears, she heard no further sounds.

After a moment a faint splashing noise carried across the water and Roisin turned around again. The sound was repeated, and as it came closer Roisin realised that it was the dipping of oars as Commandant Flanagan rowed towards her. *Thank God for that*, she thought. But where was the submarine? Commandant Flanagan had explained that it would come closer to shore before surfacing. So far nothing had appeared, though, and Roisin began to dread their plan failing at the last moment. Supposing the submarine had been depth-charged? Or forced from its course by *Kriegsmarine* destroyers? Or simply delayed for any one of a number of reasons? No, she admonished herself, fretting would get her nowhere. Commandant Flanagan trusted the Allies to provide a submarine on schedule, and she trusted Commandant Flanagan. *She had to keep her nerve.*

Forcing her fears aside, she said a quick final prayer. Then she prepared to board, as Commandant Flanagan shipped the oars and the boat crunched to a halt on the waterline shingle.

Dennis knew he had to tread carefully. Kevin Burke wasn't a fighter by nature, but he clearly cared for Roisin Tierney, and he had sounded angry when Dennis had taunted him about Vogts getting his hands on her. But was he capable of pulling the trigger? When it came to it, would he really have the stomach to shoot an unarmed opponent?

Dennis had tried a softly-softly approach, telling Kevin the *Gestapo* were on their way and that resistance was futile. The other boy hadn't been swayed, however, and Dennis was gauging what his next move should be. All of a sudden there was an eruption of water on the surface of the sea. Despite the darkness Dennis could see white waves foaming and swirling as a submarine broke the surface a couple of hundred yards out in Clifden Bay.

He couldn't believe his eyes. How on earth had someone as unimportant as Roisin Tierney been able to summon a submarine for a rescue? Because he had no doubt that that was what was planned – it was too much of a coincidence that Roisin had made her way to the shoreline exactly opposite to where the submarine had surfaced.

Even as his mind raced, he tried to calculate how to outwit Kevin. The other boy had glanced around when the submarine emerged, but he had swiftly swung back around to keep the shotgun aimed as before.

Dennis forced himself to concentrate. The submarine changed everything, creating a real risk of Roisin making a clean getaway. *He couldn't let that happen.* He hadn't come this close only to end up facing Vogts' wrath – and maybe being made the scapegoat when they were looking for someone to blame.

All wasn't lost, though. If he could take the gun from Kevin, he could fire at the small craft that would be needed for Roisin to get to the submarine. That might well be enough to scupper the rescue and force the submarine to make an emergency dive.

Making his voice sound reasonable, he took a small step forward. 'Look, Kevin, there's no point—'

'Stop right there!' interjected Kevin, moving backwards to keep the original distance between them.

'Look—'

'Shut up and listen! When I said I'd blow your head off I meant it. Don't take another step, I'm warning you.'

'OK, OK,' said Dennis, raising his hands in a gesture of surrender, but trying to gauge how serious his opponent was. He knew from experience that when it came to a fight, boys who issued warnings often wanted to avoid a clash. Was Kevin talking tough, in the hope that that would be enough to make it seem like he really would shoot? Before Dennis could calculate further, the clouds cleared again and the half-moon became visible. It illuminated the sea and the shoreline, and to Dennis's dismay revealed a rowing boat starting to make its way out to the submarine. A figure at the front of the boat was pulling strongly on the oars, and a slighter figure, that Dennis knew must be Roisin Tierney, was seated at the back.

Dennis realised that his dismay must have shown on his face, because Kevin took a swift glance over his shoulder, then immediately turned back around, the shotgun still aimed.

'So…seems like we were smarter than you after all, doesn't it?' said Kevin.

Dennis ignored the taunt. Time was running out and he had

to make a move quickly. Steeling himself to take a risk, he spoke quickly. 'I'm calling your bluff, Burke. You'd be up for murder if you shot me. But I don't think you'll do that.' Dennis took a small step forward.

Kevin moved backwards immediately, then came to a halt and looked down the barrel of the gun. 'Don't take another step. I *won't* retreat again.'

'You'll shoot me in cold blood?'

'I'll shoot you to save Roisin. Choosing between her and a snivelling little traitor is easy. And if you don't believe that, take one more step forward.'

Dennis hesitated. He had never heard Kevin Burke speak with such conviction before, and he sensed that the other boy really would shoot. 'OK,' he said, breathing out resignedly. 'OK, it's not worth dying over.'

'Good decision. Now put your hands on your head, and don't move a muscle till the submarine goes under.'

Dennis raised his hands, then started in shock. 'Oh my God! *Kommissar* Vogts!'

Kevin reacted at once, quickly spinning around.

Dennis felt a surge of exhilaration. It was the oldest trick in the book, but for the split second that mattered, Kevin had fallen for it and turned. Dennis launched himself at the other boy, colliding with him just as Kevin turned back to face him. He heard a cry of pain from his opponent as their momentum pushed him back against a stone wall. *Good*, thought Dennis, then he threw a couple of quick punches. The first one missed, but the second blow caught Kevin high on the ribcage, and Dennis was rewarded with another cry of pain.

He grabbed the barrel of the shotgun and tried to pull it from Kevin's grip. He had expected a tug of war, or for Kevin to try to punch him back. Instead of pulling away, however, Kevin went with Dennis's movement. At the last second Dennis realised what was about to happen, but by then it was too late. With the barrel pointed up in the air, Kevin used Dennis's own momentum to swing the wooden stock of the gun in a fast arc. Unable to get out of the way in time, Dennis took the full force of the blow in the stomach.

He cried out in agony and sank to his knees, completely winded. Gasping for air, Dennis struggled to rise. Before he had moved more than a couple of inches, he took another stinging blow from the gun. This one caught him squarely between the shoulder blades, and sent him sprawling face down to the ground at the gate to the field. A spasm of pain jolted through his body, made worse as Kevin rammed one foot into his back and pressed the gun hard against his head.

Dennis heard the sound of the gun being cocked and his stomach tightened in terror. 'No!' he cried. 'Don't shoot! Please!'

'I warned you!'

'Please! I won't try anything else. Don't shoot me, Kevin! Please!' Dennis felt the gun being pressed harder against his head, and his fear overcame him. 'Please,' he whimpered tearfully. 'Please...don't shoot me!' He closed his eyes, terrified that these might be his last moments on earth. Then after what seemed like an eternity the pressure of the gun against his head eased slightly.

'Here's what's going to happen,' said Kevin, his voice sounding angry but controlled. 'First of all, look down at the water and tell me what you see.'

Dennis was relieved to be still alive, but still frightened of how this would end, and he found it hard to gather himself.

'What do you see?!'

'The rowing boat…the rowing boat is getting near the sub.'

'That's right. And until they've boarded and got away safely, we stay here. If you move an inch while that's happening, I'll pull this trigger.'

Dennis felt the gun pressing harder against his head again.

'Have you any doubt about that?'

'No! No, I haven't!'

'Good,' said Kevin, slightly easing the pressure once more. 'And when they're safely gone, what will happen then?'

'I…I don't know.'

'I'll tell you what *won't* happen,' said Kevin. 'You won't say a word about this to Vogts. Because if he heard you got to within yards of Roisin and let her slip through your fingers he'd go absolutely berserk. And you'd pay the price. Also, you know now I have links to the Resistance. So if anything happens me, or anyone I know, they'll come for you. Have you any doubts about *that*?'

'No. No, I haven't.'

'Good. So you just tell Vogts that nobody knows where Roisin vanished to. She disappeared around five and wasn't seen after that.

Probably she'd been secretly planning to use this holiday for her getaway. Have you got all that?'

'Yes.'

'When we leave here, I go back to the campsite first, you follow five minutes later. With all the excitement of the fire, we'll hardly have been missed. And you *never, ever,* say a word about this. And if you value your miserable life, find a way to stop working with the *Gestapo.*'

Dennis swallowed hard. His sense of relief at not being shot was being replaced now by a feeling of despair. The events of tonight had turned his world upside down and he knew things would never be the same again. Before he could think about it any further, Kevin spoke again.

'Have a good look. That's one less Jew for your Nazi friends to persecute.'

Dennis looked out across the water and saw that the rowing boat had been abandoned. Roisin Tierney and the man who had done the rowing were climbing the conning tower of the submarine, closely followed by a crewman who quickly closed the hatch after himself. Immediately the vessel began to submerge, and within seconds all that was visible was the rowing boat and a swirling turbulence on the surface of the water.

Dennis felt the shotgun being removed from his head and the pressure of Kevin's foot eased from his back.

'Five minutes,' said Kevin dismissively, then he walked off without another word.

Dennis slowly got to his feet. His stomach ached, and his back throbbed with pain. Worst of all though was the sense of humiliation and defeat. He looked out across Clifden Bay, aware that Roisin Tierney had outwitted him. Never feeling more dejected in his life, he waited until five minutes had passed, then he began the slow trudge home.

CHAPTER TWENTY-THREE

Mary sipped a glass of tepid lemonade and gazed out the carriage window at the sunlit countryside, aware that the atmosphere around her was unusually subdued. Normally there was a sense of excitement when the youth club members travelled as a group, but the usual high spirits seemed dampened now as the train rattled along the tracks on the journey back to Dublin. Maybe it was the fact that the holiday was almost over, she thought. The trip had also been affected by the drama of Roisin's disappearance, and the subsequent questioning of all the campers by the *Gestapo* had taken some of the fun out of the holiday too.

Mary herself had mixed feelings. She was looking forward to seeing Mam again, and she was thrilled that Roisin had escaped, yet she was saddened by the knowledge that she would miss both Roisin and Dad. But she was also quietly proud of herself, for having kept her nerve during intensive questioning by *Kriminalkommissar* Vogts.

The *Gestapo* officer had arrived about an hour after the submarine escape the previous Sunday night, and had turned the campsite upside down in an angry search that became increasingly abusive when Roisin wasn't located. The next morning he had individually questioned every member of the youth club, and had given Mary, as Roisin's tent-mate, a particularly aggressive grilling.

Mary and Kevin had decided on their story, however, and Mary had stuck rigidly to the agreed line that she hadn't seen Roisin since five o'clock the previous day, and that she had no inkling either of her escape plan or of her Jewish identity. Dennis O'Sullivan had sung dumb, as Kevin predicted he would, and eventually the Nazis had left the campsite without making any arrests.

Several days later Mary had received a postcard from her mother, hoping that she was enjoying the camping, and assuring her that all family and friends were well. Mary had realised this last reference was a coded way of saying that Dad and Roisin had reached Iceland safely, and she had felt hugely relieved.

There was no telling when they would all be together again, but she resolved to pray hard each night for the Allied victory that would allow both her father and her friend to return home. To Mary, the Nazis represented all that was wrong in the world, and she clung to the belief that eventually the human spirit would prevail, and good would triumph over evil. Meanwhile, she would fight the battle, one day at a time, as best she could.

'Penny for your thoughts,' said Kevin, from the seat opposite her.

Mary put down her glass of lemonade. 'Just thinking about the future. And absent friends...'

'Right,' said Kevin.

He nodded, and Mary knew that he was aware of what she meant.

'Actually, my dad says that sometimes as a toast,' he added. 'Why don't we do that?' He raised an almost empty glass of lemonade from the table. 'To absent friends, and...and a better future.'

'To absent friends and a better future,' said Mary. She raised her glass in a toast, smiled at Kevin, then sat back contentedly as the train trundled through the sunlit countryside toward Dublin and home.

EPILOGUE

After the Allies liberated Ireland, Roisin returned from Iceland. She was reunited with her mother who had survived her time in the concentration camp on Spike Island. Roisin's father, however, never came back from the Nazi labour camp, and was found to have been buried in a mass grave in Germany. Aunt Nuala survived her period of hiding in Mayo. She moved back to Dublin when the war ended and returned to her job in the civil service, where she worked happily and uneventfully until she retired. Roisin went on to study medicine, specialising in psychiatry, and she worked for many years with people who were traumatised by their experiences during the war. She remained friends with Mary and Kevin for the rest of her life.

After the eventual Allied victory, *Kriminalkommissar* Heinrich Vogts was arrested. He was brought before the court at the Nuremberg Trials that had been set up to examine war crimes. Vogts was tried, found guilty, and executed.

Commandant Flanagan was decorated for his work with the Resistance, and he rejoined the Irish army, rising in time to become a general. Mary and her mother were also awarded medals for their bravery and sacrifices during the years of Nazi occupation. Mary became a teacher, working for all of her career in schools around Dublin. She never spoke of her wartime experiences, and none of her pupils ever knew that their good-humoured and easy-going teacher had once taken on the Nazis and won.

Dennis O'Sullivan was found drowned in the Royal Canal. After the liberation word had got out regarding his collaboration with the *Gestapo*, and there were rumours that his death was not accidental. No witnesses ever came forward, however, and nobody was ever convicted of killing him.

Kevin's mother continued to teach the violin, only finally retiring when she reached her eightieth birthday. Mr Burke continued working as an auctioneer, but lost his seat on Dublin Corporation and was never re-elected. Many people felt that he had worked too closely with the Germans during the occupation, although Roisin always credited him with saving her life by making the telephone call that warned her about Vogts. Kevin became a journalist, writing for major newspapers and magazines during a long and successful career. He covered many topics, but never wrote about what happened with Mary and Roisin during the war. They were memories, he maintained, that belonged to the three people who had lived through it. There was no need to record their story – it was something they would remember, and be proud of, all the days of their lives.

HISTORICAL NOTE

Although *Resistance* is a work of fiction and the Nazi occupation of Ireland never actually took place, it could well have become a reality. France, Belgium, The Netherlands, Poland, Russia, and many other countries were occupied by the Nazis, and in 1940 the German High Command drew up a plan for the invasion of Ireland, called Operation Green.

Under the plan, German infantry, artillery and commando units would sail from the French ports of Lorient, Saint-Nazaire and Nantes, to be landed on Ireland's south-east coast between Wexford and Dungarvan. Over 50,000 troops were expected to be used in the invasion.

Operation Green was to be closely linked to Operation Sealion, the Nazi plan to invade Britain, but after the Royal Air Force won the Battle of Britain, giving the Allies air superiority, Operation Green and Operation Sealion were both shelved.

Aside from the fictional occupation of Britain and Ireland in autumn 1940, the other historical events described are real, and the Battle of Stalingrad, the American victories against the Japanese in the Pacific, and the Battle of Kursk – the largest tank battle in history – all took place as described.

Kevin, Mary, Roisin, Dennis and their families are fictitious, as is the youth club run by Mr Cox.

Clifden is an actual town on Ireland's Atlantic seaboard, but Westwind Estate, where the youth club members camped, is fictitious. Much of Dublin has changed since 1943, and the lands surrounding Broombridge House, just east of the 7th Lock, are now the site of Glasnevin Industrial Park, while the nearby Liffey Junction has been developed as part of the Luas transport system. Shandon Park – a real location in Phibsboro – has altered little, and Prospect Cemetery and the Botanic Gardens still look similar to how they appeared in the nineteen forties.

Brian Gallagher,
Dublin, 2019.

Turn the page to read an extract from
Brian Gallagher's World War II story, *Secrets and Shadows*

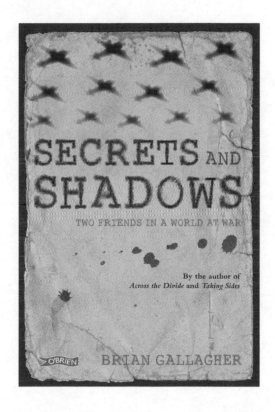

CHAPTER ONE

4 JUNE 1941, DUBLIN.

Uncle Freddie wasn't funny, but unfortunately he thought he was. He was sitting at the breakfast table and imitating Mr Churchill, the British Prime Minister. Grace wanted to tell him that he didn't sound a bit like the English leader, whom she had often seen on the Movietone News at the cinema. She bit her tongue. Ma had warned her not to complain about anything. Ma said that guests had to adapt to their hosts, not the other way round, and that they must be good house guests while they were staying with Granddad and his son, Uncle Freddie.

Grace loved Granddad, who was soft-spoken and kind. Even Uncle Freddie wasn't too bad when he acted like the electrician that he was, instead of trying to be a comedian. To Grace's relief he ended his impersonation of Mr Churchill, acknowledged their polite laughter, and returned to his breakfast porridge, slurping it slightly in a way that Grace found annoying.

'More tea, anyone?' said Ma.

'Thanks, Nancy, don't mind if I do,' said Granddad.

'Freddie?'

'Sure a bird never flew on one wing, what?' said Freddie, holding out his teacup for Ma to pour.

'You might as well have a hot sup too, love,' said Ma, and Grace nodded in agreement.

Like most twelve-year-olds she wasn't particularly keen on tea, but because of the war it was rationed, so adults hated wasting it once a pot had been made.

They all drank up, and Grace thought how strange it was to be staying here. A week ago she had been living contentedly with Ma in their cottage. She wished that they could return there right this minute. But Ma had always taught her to be positive, so she stopped thinking about how they had been left homeless and tried to feel grateful for the roof over their heads.

'Did I tell you I got three ounces of tobacco last night?' said Uncle Freddie proudly, like this was a big achievement.

'Really?' answered Ma politely.

'Leave it to Freddie, what?!' her uncle continued, happily praising himself.

Great, thought Grace, now he'll be smoking his smelly pipe

even more.

'How did you manage that?' asked Granddad.

Granddad wasn't a pipe smoker himself, but Grace had noticed that adults were usually intrigued when someone managed to get extra supplies of the things that were scarce because of the war.

'Oh now...' said Freddie, as though he were some kind of man of mystery. Then he couldn't resist boasting and he looked at Grace and winked. 'You scratch my back,' he said.

'Sorry?'

'You scratch my back, and I'll scratch yours.'

'Right...'

Freddie turned to the others now, like a magician revealing a very clever trick.

'Didn't I wire the tobacconist's house last year, and did him a few extra sockets. So I dropped into his shop last night and told him I was gummin' for a smoke.'

'Very subtle, Freddie,' said Granddad with a grin.

'Subtle gets you nowhere. Ask and you shall receive – amn't I right, Nancy?'

'I'm sure you are,' said Ma agreeably.

Maybe I could ask him to stop slurping his porridge, thought Grace – though I know what I'd receive if I did!

'What's the joke?' said Freddie.

Grace realised that she must have been smiling to herself. Freddie looked at her enquiringly, and she tried not to panic.

'Eh...just...just thinking about a Mutt and Jeff cartoon,' she

265

answered. Mutt and Jeff were cartoon characters in the Evening Herald newspaper, and they were the first thing that came into her head.

'Ah yeah, those lads would make a cat laugh, right enough,' said Freddie, and Grace felt relieved that he accepted her answer.

'Talking about cats,' said Freddie, 'Did I tell you about the aul' wan with the cats in Terenure?'

'You did, yeah,' said Granddad.

'I didn't tell you though, Nancy, did I?'

'No,' answered Ma, and Grace could see that even someone as good natured as Ma had to make an effort to seem eager for one of Freddie's tales this early in the morning. 'What was that, Freddie?' she asked gamely.

Freddie put down his bowl of porridge and leaned forward. 'It's a good one, if I say so myself...'

Freddie began telling a long-winded story, and Grace followed Ma's example, trying for an interested look on her face. Inside she felt differently. Why do we have to be here?, she thought, as she wished, with all her heart, that she was back home where she belonged.

★★★

Barry was worried. The class bully, Shay McGrath, had been picking on him during the three weeks that he had been attending his new school in Ireland. Going in the entrance gate a moment

266

ago McGrath had suddenly pushed him for no reason, and Barry feared that today would be a bad day.

It had started off discouragingly when he saw the headline of the newspaper that was delivered to his grandma's house each morning. The paper said that the Greek island of Crete had just fallen to the Nazis, and Barry wondered how the Germans could be stopped as they swept across Europe. What hope was there of his Uncle George being set free from the prisoner of war camp where he was held, unless the Nazis were defeated? And Barry knew that his own father wouldn't get to come home from the Royal Navy unless the Allies won the war and defeated Adolf Hitler.

It was now over eight months since Dad had been home on leave. It seemed like ages ago, and Barry wished they could be together again. He missed the funny songs that Dad sang to make him laugh, and going to football matches together at Anfield, and just having him around the house. But his father's ship was still in action somewhere in the Mediterranean and there was no telling when they would see each other.

Barry missed his mother too, even though it was only three and a half weeks since she had sent him off to Dublin. After the night when they had brought the old woman to the underground shelter Mum had insisted that for safety's sake he go and stay with his grandma in neutral Ireland. That night in Liverpool had been the worst of the war, and the devastation in the city centre the next day was horrific. Lewis's, the famous department store, had taken a direct hit and was gutted, and a ship loaded with a cargo of bombs had exploded in Huskisson Dock, causing such a colossal blast that the two-ton ship's anchor block landed outside Bootle Hospital, a mile and a half away.

During a week of attacks over six hundred bombers had pounded the city, devastated the docks and wrecked the Custom House, the Liverpool Museum, and many other local landmarks. Thousands of people had been killed and injured, with even more left homeless. But although the raids had been frightening, Barry still hadn't wanted to leave his friends behind.

Mum couldn't be talked out of it, though, and she had bought the ferry ticket and made all the arrangements. Barry had then argued that if Liverpool was that dangerous, she should come to Dublin too. But Mum was stubborn. She worked in a factory manufacturing aeroplane engines for the Royal Air Force, and she explained that she couldn't shirk her part in the fight against Hitler while Dad was risking his life at sea, and Uncle George was locked up in a prison camp.

He remembered her wiping away her tears and trying to keep a smile on her face as she waved him off on the ferry from Liverpool to Dublin. His Grandma Peg, Dad's Irish mother, had gone out of her way to make him feel welcome in Ireland. And he liked Dublin, and had often stayed in his grandma's house in Arbour Hill during the summer holidays. But living here was different. Taken away from his old school and his old friends, he was suddenly the new boy – and an easy target for jeering with his different background and English accent.

He walked into the school yard, the sky overcast, and he nodded to several boys from his class who were gathering for the Tuesday morning drill session with their Polish instructor, Mr Pawlek. Not all the boys in his class were mean to him, and Barry's ability to tell jokes had broken the ice with some of his classmates. But he understood how schoolyards worked, and if a bully like McGrath decided he didn't like someone, then McGrath's gang would go along with it – as would other boys who didn't want to get on the wrong side of a bully.

On Barry's first day in the school McGrath had loudly asked was it not enough to have the English coming over to Ireland for 700 years – without another one of them moving into sixth class. Barry had kept his voice reasonable and answered that thousands of Irish people had been glad to go to England, people like his own dad, who as a young man couldn't find work in Ireland.

McGrath had sneered and said, 'Fine. Let's do a swap. Your aul' fella can come back to Ireland – and you go back to England!'

Some of the other boys had laughed, but Barry had shrugged it off, not wanting to get into a fight with a bigger, intimidating character like McGrath. The annoying thing was that he would have happily gone back to Liverpool in the morning. But he had no choice; his mother had insisted that he had to stay in Dublin.

So here he was, three weeks into his time in Brunner – St Paul's Boys' School in Brunswick Street – with almost four weeks to go before the term ended. He crossed the school yard, the air heavy with the smell from the nearby soap factory. Today was the first school day since the weekend air raid on Dublin's North Strand, and many of the boys were talking about how the Germans had bombed the city, despite Ireland being a neutral country.

'Did you hear the explosions at the weekend?' asked Charlie Dawson, a slight but perky boy who was friendly to Barry when McGrath wasn't around.

'Yes,' answered Barry, 'they woke us up.'

'I heard the army were firing up green, white and orange flares – so the pilot would know he was over Ireland.'

'Really?'

'That's what they're saying,' said Charlie. 'Didn't work though, did it?'

'No, I suppose not.'

'My da went down there the next day. Said the damage was desperate – he never saw anything like it.'

He should have seen Liverpool, thought Barry, though he was careful not to say it. Although the attack by one aeroplane on Dublin was tiny compared to the massive raids on his hometown, it was still terrible for the people who had been killed and injured at the North Strand.

'All right, boys, form a line!' said McGrath as he approached. He said it in imitation of the foreign accent of Mr Pawlek, and the other boys laughed at McGrath's mimicry.

Even though he didn't want to antagonise the class bully, Barry couldn't bring himself to join in. For one thing Mr Pawlek was fair-minded and popular – and he had been particularly welcoming to Barry as a new boy. There was also the fact that Barry too had a different accent to the rest of the boys, so he wouldn't make fun of the drill teacher's grammatically correct but accented English.

McGrath approached Barry, aware that he wasn't laughing. 'No sense of humour, Malone?'

Barry wasn't going to apologise for not going along with the joke, but neither did he want to provoke the bigger boy, so he said nothing.

'Anyone ever tell you that?' persisted McGrath.

Still Barry refused to be drawn, and now McGrath sneered and mimicked his Liverpool accent.

'Anyone ever tell you there's something wrong with the talking part of your brain?' he said.

'Anyone ever tell you you're a pain?' snapped Barry, unable to take any more goading.

Several of the other boys looked surprised, and Charlie Dawson said 'That even rhymes!'

'Yeah we get it, Dawson,' said McGrath, aggressively turning on him.

'I'm…I'm only saying,' answered Charlie.

'Well, don't say. And you, Malone,' said McGrath, turning to Barry. 'Think you're smart, don't you?'

Barry racked his brains for an answer that wouldn't sound like giving in, but that also wouldn't make things worse.

'Everything all right, boys?' said a voice, then Mr Pawlek casually stepped between them. He was muscularly built, with sandy brown hair and clear blue eyes, and he moved with the ease of a natural athlete.

'Everything is fine, sir,' said Barry with relief.

Mr Pawlek looked enquiringly at McGrath, who held his gaze briefly, then nodded.

'Yeah, fine, sir,' he said.

'Right, put aside your bags and form a line,' said the drill teacher.

Barry turned away from McGrath without another word and placed his schoolbag against the wall. This time he had been saved by Mr Pawlek, and with luck the incident might blow over. But he sensed that his smart answer had made McGrath more of an enemy than ever, and he feared there would be trouble ahead.